JOY OF WOMANHOOD

Flourish is a very beautiful and dazzling woman who had never had peace in her marriage. She couldn't bear a child for her husband because of her previous life. In a Nigerian marriage any woman who is unable to bear a child is considered a barren woman and is expected to leave her husband's house. She is considered barren and unfaithful and that was why she wasn't able to bear a child.

Flourish's mother in law had pressurized her husband to leave her and marry another woman but because of the love David has for his wife he refused to listen to his mother's contemplations. Flourish wanted to do everything possible to save her marriage. She knew that her mother in law hated her and would do anything to get her out.

She went to meet a doctor who told her that she was infertile and that her womb was really damaged as a result of the many abortions she had in the past.

To flourish all hope were lost for her in her husband's family. She started crying. " so what do you mean doctor; that I can never bear a child". She said as some tears dropped down her cheeks." Yes ma, your womb is considered invulnerable as a result of the abortions you had and have rendered your womb weak and now no fetus can grow in that womb". The doctor said feeling pity for her.

'But all hope isn't lost, why don't you just adopt a child'. He asked feeling that it would be the perfect idea. 'No sir that is not possible my mother in law has the belief that adopted children are always wayward and that she doesn't want to raise a wayward child''. She said still crying. "Wow, but I don't think there's a solution to your problem". The doctor said facing the other side of the room.

Flourish had no choice but to go home hopeless. While she was in the bus she started reflecting and thinking about her previous life. She came from a poor home. Her dad was a community farmer. He worked for a very rich man.

The man had a very big farm almost 4 hectare of land. He employed most of the villagers who were looking for work among which her father was included .He employed them to work and cultivate the crops and at the end of each harvest, each farmer is paid twenty thousand naira.

The money they were paid was too small compared to the work they were doing. Anyway he had to make do with it. Justin, Flourish mother was a tailor. Sometimes after school, Flourish would come to her mother's shop to help her with some work.

At that time Justine had no apprentice so whenever she was going to Onitsha to buy some good quality materials she always put flourish in charge. On one occasion when Flourish was busy arranging the store. Bella, her classmate came and was surprised seeing her at a tailors shop. 'E….shoo since when did you start learning tailoring'. Bella said surprised. "No I'm not learning tailoring, my mum is the owner of this shop but she is not around so she told me to stay and watch the shop". Flourish said sweeping the floor. "Leave that job, please just follow me out,

I'm going for some shopping". Bella said pleading. Flourish dropped the broom and turned to where Bella was standing.

"What are you saying, shopping, with which person's money"? Flourish asked a little bit surprised because she knew that Bella's parents were not that rich at least they were average.

"My sister you are still in the dark, my boyfriend spends on me every day, check me out". She said turning around. "Boy?" Flourish asked even more surprised. "Yes boyfriend and on top of that I have a sugar daddy". She said bringing out her phone. "Shoo who bought you a phone?" Flourish asked even more mesmerized. 'my sister who else except my boyfriend, like I said he spends on me every day, today he gave me a hundred thousand naira to go shopping and I really do not want to do this alone'. She said looking at Flourish.

"My sister I'm sorry but I cannot go with you because my mother placed me in charge of her store and I really don't want to disappoint her". Flourish said picking up her broom and continued her sweeping.

“Flourish please we won’t be late I will only take thirty minutes and before you know it we would be back, I promise” Bella said lying. ‘Are you sure’ Flourish asked wanting to follow her. ‘Of course I’m sure why would I lie again and it would even be in your favor because I will give you some money to also buy what you want’. Bella said smiling. Flourish agreed and the both of them helped in packing the things in the store up. Flourish followed Bella to a shopping mall just down the streets. Flourish was shocked by the kind of clothes Bella was buying. She was buying clothes that exposed her growing body.

Bella naturally had a fine physique with big bust and buttocks. Most of the boys at school had fallen for her. Flourish was in SS3 and only fifteen years old. She was just shopping nets; half cuts shirts, with bum shots that showed off half of her buttocks. She also shopped for rugged jeans and some tight pants. She even bought all those swimming pants that were tokened inside their buttocks.

‘What are all these you are buying’. Flourish asked really very shocked. “What do they look like to you?" She said angry with the question. "I know that you are just shopping but where do you intend on wearing this clothes to" She said a little bit confused.

"How many times do I have to tell you that I have a boyfriend as well as a sugar daddy"? She said really upset with the question.

"No more questions, just buy exactly what I'm buying, I'll pay for it' she was really tired of Flourish. "But my parents will never allow me put this clothing on". Flourish said picking them up one by one and nodded her head in disgust.

"Flourish I'm really making a lot of money from this my sugar daddy". "Shoo really…." She asked really amused please tell me how". Flourish asked really interested.

"My sugar daddy pays me thirty thousand naira every day for spending the night with him and so does my boyfriend, every week I get almost two hundred thousand naira to enjoy my life".

Flourish was speechless. She never knew that Bella was this rich. She wanted to join by all means. "Ah see, I really need some money to help my family, if you can earn that big amount of money with what you are doing then I suppose I can also be rich" Flourish said really very happy.

"Yes Na and anyway my boyfriend has a friend who really wants a girl, if you can I will take you there". Bella said.

"I know but look at what I'm wearing''. Flourish said looking at herself. Her outfit was really dirty. "Don't worry about that, take these clothes''. She said bringing out a jeans and blue polo. "Here you go, take this to the changing room and put it on".

Flourish did exactly what Bella said, and the clothes really looked fitted on her. Bella paid for the clothes and they both went to Bella's boyfriend house.

Flourish was really scared. She didn't know if she was doing the right thing or not. On getting to Travis house which was the name of Bella's boyfriend, Flourish couldn't believe her eyes.

The boy was living in a mansion. "Wow this boyfriend of yours is a rich guy". Flourish said as her eyes almost plucked out of her socket. She was so mesmerized by what she saw.

For once she knew that Bella was really enjoying.

When they entered the house, it was a mess. It was as if they had a night party. “Was there a night party here?” Asked flourish who was disgusted at the sight of alcohol bottles scattered round the house and some ladies underwear.

“Yes there was a night party.” Bella answered shyly because her underwear was also among those littered round the house.

Before Flourish could ask another question, Travis came downstairs. “Wow babe, you’re here.” He said as he kissed her. Flourish couldn’t believe what she just witnessed.

Truly the desire of men had really covered up their eyes. She was so shocked seeing her friend kissing a guy at her very young age. She was barely 17.

She then believed that Bella would go to any extent to get money even if it means having sex with a man that was old enough to become her grandfather. She was just in her world of imagination when Bella interrupted.

"Anyway babe, this is Flourish and she is in dying need of a boyfriend. I was hoping you could hook her up with that your friend." Bella said like a rat begging the cat for a small piss of cheese.

"No problem my friend is coming over, maybe they could talk and get to know each other and anyway hi." He said as he turned to Flourish requesting for a hand shake.

That was it. That was how Flourish got to know henry.

She started putting on skimpy clothes that exposed her growing body, all in the name of money, but flourish didn't know that the consequences were devastating.

Flourish's parents had noticed that she was no longer holy and that she had been negatively influenced. Her mother decided to talk to her. She wanted to know the part she had failed as a mother. One cool evening when flourish was receiving the cool breeze under the tree browsing, Justine, her mother thought it was the right time to talk to her daughter. "My child, you and I know that where you are heading is darkness. You know the adage that says what an elderly person sees while sitting down; a young person will climb a tree but still won't see it. My daughter please stops whatever you are doing." She said feeling pity for her poor daughter.

She knew her daughter to be a very good and decent girl. Both she and her husband had really instilled good behavior into their daughter. She wondered how a girl of qualities could easily go down the drain.

"Mama what is this stupid proverb you are preaching to me this evening. Is it because I've been keeping quiet all this while? " flourish said really angry as she got up and left. Normally, flourish was never rude but one thing about being influenced is that you slowly but gradually become like the person who influenced you.

Her mother just nodded her head in pity; she knew that her daughter had been sucked up by the devil. The demons had blind folded her making it impossible for her to see the big port hole right in front of her.

After about some months, Flourish started feeling nausea and she vomited almost every seconds. Even at the slightest aroma of her food she would go and throw up. Her mother suspected what the symptoms could be but she didn't want to just jump into conclusion.

Her father was really angry with her but he just didn't want to throw his anger on her, there is a saying "many days for the thief one day for the owner". He was waiting patiently for the day when her cup would be full.

Three days after that incident occurred, flourish fainted while washing her clothes outside. Her parents quickly rushed her to the hospital only to get the suspense of their life.

"Doctor please, how is my daughter." Justine asked in a tone that represented fear. She was really tensed. "Calm down she's fine but I'm afraid to say that she is two weeks pregnant." The doctor said.

Now Flourish's father was super angry. He had been really holding up his anger but not for long. "I knew that idiot would not let me have peace and I really can't tolerate her nonsense behavior." He said really angry. He had just disowned his own daughter.

"You couldn't take good care of your stupid daughter now look what she has done to this family. I'm afraid to say that from now on Flourish is not my daughter". He said addressing his wife.

He told his daughter face to face that he wanted her to leave his house which she gladly did. She didn't waste a second before leaving the hospital.

She quickly went to meet the father of her child but it seems that he was never ready to become a father so soon.

"Honey" as that was the name she usually addressed her boyfriend, Henry. "What is it babe, do you want a drink". He asked because he already knew the reason why she must have come.

"Honey, look we have a very big problem at our hands". She said wanting to cry.

He then placed his hand on her shoulder and raised her jaw up. “Alright tell me what the problem is”. He said heading towards the fridge to collect a bottle of brandy. “Honey, I’m pregnant”. She said releasing the bullet.

“What are you saying? this is absolute nonsense. I’m not the father of your child please get the hell out of here.” He said really angry as he showed Flourish the way to the door. She was shocked on hearing that Henry denied responsibility of her unborn baby.

How could men be so deceptive, they take advantage of poor girls and refuse to accept their unborn baby? Flourish who had been hoping that her boyfriend would accept her pregnancy had to go back heartbroken.

She knew her father had already disowned her and there was no way she could go back; she had no place to go to. After some close thoughts within her she went to Bella’s house only to be embarrassed by her very own best friend.

She felt that her best friend would take her in but it was a whole different chapter.

"Bella I have a very big problem at hand, and I want you to help me out." flourish said feeling sober. Her heart had been really broken. The scales that were in her eyes had finally fallen and now she was regretting ever making such a mistake.

"Tell me what it is, my guy isn't around and I want to prepare something for him to eat before he arrives." She said.

"Look I'm pregnant, and now my boyfriend has denied responsibility of the child. He sent me out of his house and on the other hand my dad has disowned me, he does not consider me his daughter anymore. I have no place to go now that's why I want to live here." She said innocently.

Bella had her own life to live she wasn't ready to take care of another person. So she quickly refused the offer

"Look girl, how does this one bother me, I mean I'm not the one who got you pregnant so why are you coming to me?" She said rudely.

Flourish could not believe her eyes. The one who brought her into this mess was running away from her. She was so upset and angry with herself for ever falling into that bloody trap.

On the other hand she just couldn't take care of the pregnancy all by herself. She then turned to abortion as the only key to escape a lot of embarrassment.

She then travelled to Lagos after carrying out the abortion, but in order to earn money to take care of her and live up to standards, she then turned to prostitution.

She never knew that she was causing herself more problems. She also got pregnant for different men and she also aborted the pregnancies which made her womb weak.

It was in the process of her carrying out this abortion that she met her darling husband but their relationship was never meant to be permanent since she couldn't bear a child for her husband.

If only she had not followed the way of Bella she would have been blessed with children and she would have been living happily with her husband. While in the bus recalling her whole life, she started pitying her husband. She still could not believe that there was no hope for her and meanwhile the Bella who she was trying to emulate was already blessed with triplets. She had already gotten married 2 years ago and she had the kids the previous year.

She started saying to herself, "what have I done to myself? How will I tell my husband that there is no hope of us having children? How will I tell him that as a result of my stupid behavior in the past we can't have a child now?" She said talking to herself. It was only her lips that were moving; her voice could not be heard.

The woman sitting beside her noticed it and decided to talk to her. "My Sister I hope all is well?" The woman asked really concerned.it was clear that she was not in a good mood.

"My sister no…. I'm having problems in my marital life". Flourish replied sad. She sounded like she had just lost a family member. The woman was really touched by the way flourish sounded.

"What is the problem, feel free to share your problems with me." The woman said placing her hand on her chest which meant that she was really concerned.

"My sister I'm infertile, and I'm trying my very best to have a child for my husband but it seems that all my efforts are in vain. My mother-in-law has been really determined to kick me out of the house". She said hissing with pain in her words.

Tears dropped down her cheeks as thoughts of her past life kept on hunting her.

The woman really felt her pain. "Hum". She sighed thinking of ideas in other to help Flourish. "My sister, if that is the case why not adopt a child?" The woman said feeling that would be the right thing to do. "That's where you're getting it wrong, my mother in law believes that adopted children are always bad and are involved in antisocial behavior."

To flourish all hope was lost; she knew that the only thing to do now was to patiently wait for divorce papers. She knew that her mother-in-law would have been pressurizing her husband to file for a divorce.

“Yes”. Faithful shouted like someone who was told of an answer and quickly remembered it.

“My sister what happened” Flourish asked curiously as if Faithful had found a solution to her problem.

“I’ve gotten a solution to your problem, there’s this pastor I know about who is very good at helping childless couples have children. I think you should try him”. She said in a helpful manner.

Flourish had no idea with what she was dealing with. At first she hated going to see pastors but she just had to see the pastor.

“But do I know him? I mean is he a popular pastor.” She asked a little bit scared and security conscious. She didn’t want to fall for all those fake pastors.

“Yes he is a very popular pastor, everybody knows about him, I will give you the name of his church and the address so that you can spare sometime to see him.” Faithful said as she quickly brought out a piece of paper and wrote all what she knows about the pastor.

Flourish had no choice, though she never believed in any of these miracles performed by these pastors she just had to try her best. They parted ways after arriving at their different locations. Flourish started thinking about what Faithful had said, she didn't want to stress herself too much so she decided to go the next day.

Chapter 2

When flourish finally got home, the drama began; her mother in law was at home and so wanted to start trouble with her. "Madam, what are you still doing here? You can't give my son a child of his own and yet you are still cheating on him, what kind of a heartless woman are you?" Rita, David's mother said in absolute disgust.

"Mama what is this drama you are acting, why can't you just let the sleeping dog lie? Do you always have to create drama out of any slightest issue on ground?" David said so angrily with his mother. Flourish was just watching as both mother and son were fighting.

She always said to herself that she was the cause of the disunity that had befallen the family.

David angrily left the sitting room and headed to his room while flourish followed.

She didn't want anything to do with her mother in law. As she got to the room, she saw her husband sitting in the bed in a position that signifies frustration.

Flourish did feel pity for her husband; she wished that God would make things normal again.

"Honey I know how frustrated you are but I'm trying my best. I'm doing everything possible to enable us have children." She said assuring him. She was sure that one day God would eventually bless her with children. "It is not like I'm frustrated. My mother just keeps on making matters worse. Instead of her to try and encourage me and strengthen my faith she just keeps on fuelling the issue on ground. David said really exhausted.

Flourish could understand clearly what was in her husband's mind, she decided to comfort him.

"Honey there is nothing to worry about, I went to see a doctor this afternoon and he told me that there might be hope." She said lying. She just wanted her husband to be rest assured.

"Really, this means that we would become parents very soon." He said so excited. He believed the silly lie told by his wife. Flourish didn't want to raise false hope for her husband so she prayed to God in her hearts that the plan be successful.

The next day, she hurriedly left the house; she didn't want anything galloping in her plans for the day.

She used the address given by Faithful and she found herself in Rock of Ages Ministries. It was then she remembered the pastor and all the miracles he had performed.

There was a pregnant woman who could not put to birth for over 2 years now. The husband of the woman had taken her to so many doctors who said that there was nothing wrong with her medically.

The man suspected that it was a spiritual thing and so decided to bring her to pastor Clifford Igiebor.

Pastor Clifford then told the man that there was something blocking his wife's womb and that was why she couldn't bear the child.

He said that the enemies had planted something in her womb and that was why she couldn't give birth to the child. According to the pastor, the child was to be born to solve most of the world's problem but the devil doesn't want that to happen.

It was said that the pastor actually healed the woman but the hidden misery behind her healing was still untold. It was said that the woman was threatened not to ever reveal what the pastor eventually did to her on that Faithfull day.

Flourish already knew what the pastor must have done to the poor innocent woman.It was clear that the pastor actually slept with the woman because why would he have ever threatened the woman not to ever reveal what he did to her.

She started thinking about what the pastor would do to her as she entered the church. The church was really big and beautiful. She was just admiring the church when a woman came to tap her.

"Hello madam, how may I help you?" the woman asked seeing that flourish was new there.

"Well I want to see the pastor of this church." She replied shyly.

"Please madam, be specific in your words. We have a lot of pastors in this church so which one do you want to see?" The woman asked politely. She was the choir mistress.

Flourish didn't know any pastor there in the church, but there was one pastor she knew quite well and that was Pastor Clifford.

"Well can I see Pastor Clifford?" She asked stammering.

The woman told her that the pastor was not around at the moment but she should enjoy the first service before he arrives. Flourish had no choice, she decided to wait. Though she was used to going to church she did enjoyed the service. Few minutes after the service, the pastor arrived. He was an incredibly huge and handsome guy.

He was properly dressed to deliver his sermon on the pulpit on the second service. He saw Flourish walking majestically towards him. To him he had seen a beautiful angel whom was sent by God to bless him that cold morning.

"Good morning sir, my name is Flourish." She said requesting for a handshake. The pastor was so delighted to see such a beauty.

"Please my child do well to come into my office, the lord is with you." The pastor said placing his hand on her head and bringing her into his office.

"Please do take a seat my child, this is the first time I'm having a guest since the beginning of this month." The pastor said laughing. The way he laughed was so strange but she ignored it.

"So my dear what brings you here?" He asked still looking at her. "Well sir I'm having problems in my marriage, I mean I can't bear a child for my husband. I've been going to so many doctors but none of them can solve my problem, that's why I came here" she said in a distress mood.

"Hmm." The pastor sighed. "Well my child this is a spiritual thing but don't worry, when there is life there is hope. God always have a way of helping people."

After hearing what the pastor had said she started having hope towards the future. The pastor looked at her from head to toe, she was very beautiful. God had really blessed her with a fine physique "My child God has sent me to help you but you will have to do something. It is what God demands."

Flourish didn't understand what the pastor meant. "Sir what does God demand? I will do anything god says." She said really determined.

"Look my dear, God has said that I should sleep with you, I'm sorry it is the only way."

On hearing that Flourish jumped out of her seat in anger. She couldn't believe that the pastor would stoop that low to do such a disgusting thing.

"What are you saying sir? You don't expect me to sleep with you" she said in anger. Now she was sure that all the miracles that he had been performing on all those women were all lies. He was only sleeping with them for his own selfish interest.

The pastor was trying to make Flourish understand but she was not ready to just give in. her past experiences had really shown her a lot of lessons. One of the lessons was to never trust a guy.

"My dear, I'm telling you that God never lies. He has told me to do this to you. He has given me the power already and it is in my manhood. Try to see through God. He said trying to convince him but she was wiser than the pastor.

"You are a useless man. I can't believe that you will say such a disgusting thing. Do you think I'm like those innocent women who you can have your way out? See let me tell you my experiences in life has really taught me a good lesson and I'm not ready to go through it again, so it's better you just look for someone else. I can't believe that I'm actually talking to this fool." She said in disgust.

The pastor knew that it would be difficult to convince Flourish so he decided to let her go. Flourish on the other hand regretted ever coming to the church but she was so confuse because she had no idea what to do next.

While thinking outside the church, she received a call. It was from her uncle. She was so happy seeing his call because it had been really long since they talked or seen each other.

Her uncle had been really there for her. Even after she got pregnant out of wedlock he still supported her. He was even the one who encouraged her to find a guy and get married to him.

She was as glad as she hurriedly picked his call.

"Ah hello, my child, how many minutes will it takes you to pick my calls." He said a little bit angry with the delay.

"Sorry uncle, but is that enough to start being angry. Well enough of that uncle; tell me how everybody is in Ibadan" she said smiling.

"Well what do you expect? We are all doing well, well tell me how are you." he asked.

Her mood began to change. She was not really happy with her life. She was trying her very best to save her very own stumbling marriage.

"Well uncle you know about the pains and sufferings I'm going through. All my efforts keep on bringing fruitless result. I'm already tired. I just can't tolerate it anymore." She said crying.

Her uncle felt her pain. He did feel pity for his poor niece but there was nothing he could about the matter.

"See my child, I know that you are passing through hard times but you and I know that there is nothing I could possibly do at the moment." He said trying to comfort her, because she still didn't stop crying.

"Look my dear, my wife is a gynecologist I can talk to her to help you but in the meantime I want you to come here. At least leave Lagos for a while and enjoy your life." On hearing that Flourish heart jumped out of excitement. Her heart was calm now that she had hope. She thanked her uncle who told her that he would make arrangements for her to come to Ibadan the next week.

Flourish was so excited. She quickly rushed home only to receive the greatest shock of her life. Her mother in law had arranged for another lady to be David's wife. She knew how stubborn Flourish was and it won't be easy to get her out of the house so she decided to bring a woman to the house to at least steal her son's heart.

After sighting Flourish from a distance she told the two love birds to sit next to each other. David considered it a pleasure. He was already falling in love with the woman his mother brought. Really that was too easy, maybe because of how beautiful she was.

Joan was a very beautiful girl. She could be considered as a village belle. Her eyes were as brown as that of a gazelle skin.

She had a very dark brown skin and it was as smooth as the skin of a young bird. Anyone who saw her at first sight would definitely fall in love with her.

Though he still loved Flourish he also wanted a child and he knew that she couldn't give a child to him so he had no choice but to agree.

Just then flourish walks in only to see her husband holding another woman and they were talking to each other happily. She knew that there was no hope anymore in her husband

She just quietly walked into her bedroom. It was as if her husband didn't notice her coming in, this made her cry, and it was as if the world hated her. All through her life she had never found true happiness. She had been trying her very best to preserve her marriage but her mother in law was still persistent in letting her leave the house.

She had no choice than to leave the house, she packed her belongings and through the back door she left. She didn't know where to go next because her uncle had told her that he would make arrangements for her to come the following week.

The only available place that came to her mind was to stay in a hotel which she eventually went to.

Meanwhile, Rita had called Joan's mother so that they could start making preparations for the wedding. She just wanted her son to get married to a woman who would produce a grandchild for her.

Few days later, her uncle invited her over to Ibadan. Flourish didn't hesitate to leave Lagos. To her Lagos had given her a lot of problems and that it was full of sorrow and depression. Her uncle had sent his wife to go pick her up from the park.

Flora was so excited to see Flourish; it had been long she last saw her.

Seeing his very own niece, he was so excited and he promised to find a job for her. After flora had taken her through the beautiful sites in Ibadan, Flourish got used to the environment and could walk on her own without getting lost.

On one occasion while she was doing her early morning jogging she encountered Travis. As she caught sight of him, she felt annoyed and irritated. She tried to leave the scene but Travis blocked her way.

"Babe, it was as if God just wanted the both of us to see each other this very good morning" he said smiling.

Flourish felt disgusted on hearing babe. In her mind she started saying to herself. 'So this man has the guts to even call me babe after all he has done to my life and marriage". She kept on saying a lot of bad things about him until he pinched her seeing that her mind was not here. It was clear that she was thinking about something because the way she was curiously looking at him was like a monkey who had seen a banana in another's monkey tree. There is a possibility that both are going to end up fighting

He feared that was what Flourish wanted to do to him. "I hope you are not angry with me" Travis asked pretending to show concern and remorseful.

Flourish just smiled and nodded her head positively. This frightened Henry because she was behaving so abnormally. "I can't actually believe that you would gather up the guts to come to me and call me your babe. I mean you are not even ashamed of all the evil that you did in the past" she said wanting to slap him.

Henry was tired of trying to sweet talk Flourish it was as if all his efforts were in vain. He decided to put in some attitude.

"Look I really don't have the time to waste here. I'm only doing these so that you can give me my child." He said looking the other way.

Flourish was shocked to hear that he still thought that their child was still alive. She began to imagine how his reactions would be if she told him that she had murdered the child so many years ago.

"Well I'm sorry to say but you have no child. I killed your child so many years ago, I didn't want to raise any child as a single mother" she said. That word sounded as a bomb shell in Henry's ears.

He wished he had not made that mistake of refusing to accept the child now he had to face the consequences of been childless forever.

Travis had now gotten married and because of his wayward life while still young, he couldn't bear a child of his own. His wife had gone to all doctors of different kind but they all said the same thing that nothing was wrong with her medically.

It began to dawn on Henry that he could have been the cause. He went to meet a native doctor who told him that he should go in search of his lost child. He then decided that he will look for Flourish. Luckily for him he saw her while doing his early morning chores. Now he was shot dead in his mind. Instead of trying to accept his mistake he kept on adding fuel to the problems that Flourish already had. "You bombastic element, how could you think of doing such a disgusting thing? You know that I played a lot of role in giving you that pregnancy and now you have the guts to remove it; what were you thinking that made you do that". He said letting out his rage.

Flourish was disgusted with the way Henry was speaking. She just pitied the woman who was living with him.

"I'm so ashamed of myself right now that I was dating a man like you. You have the guts to say that you played a big role in that pregnancy that has ruined my marital life. You are a selfish man." She said angrily and left the scene immediately.

Henry now had to bear the cross alone; as flourish got home after her morning work which was interrupted by Henry her uncle surprised her.

He had planned for Flourish to start working in an oil company, the company deals with the processing of palm oil. He thought that maybe this would keep her busy. She accepted the job offer.

The next day which was the day that Flourish was going to take her interview; her uncle gave her some advice.

"Look my dear" he said holding her forehead and drawing her hair backward.

"See I want you to live a good life, I want you to start your life afresh. There is a saying that you should never start your day with the broken pieces of yesterday. If you continue to think about that man you may never want to move on. Just take my advice and make friends. I know in my heart that you would take the job." Flourish decided that she would start her life afresh. She went for the interview, they told her that she was not qualified to be a manager but there was still a vacant space for a janitor.

This was one work Flourish disliked. Being a janitor you would have to clean each and every worker's office. That was so embarrassing. Instead of her to be in the office she would have to clean it

She didn't want to take any chance but she had no choice. She was in Ibadan and she needed to work for her money. She agreed to take the job and she left to tell her uncle about the interview. He was glad that finally she had a place to work but sooner did they know that this was he beginning of their worries and pain. Flourish life was about to change.

Chapter 3

Flourish had started working as a janitor in the oil company and she was enjoying her work until when she met Travis. She wasn't aware that he was also working there. She regretted ever working in his office. The only thing he wanted to do to her was to embarrass her.

That very fateful afternoon when she was cleaning Travis office he threw away the water she was using to clean.

Flourish became angry and yelled at him. "What is wrong with you, can't you see, why do you keep on disturbing me?" She said with anger written over her.

"I guess you did miss a spot, but I don't think you should blame me" he said smiling with a devilish face.

Flourish felt like killing him right at the spot but she had to control herself. She only blamed herself the more because it was her fault, if she had not chosen to be with a guy like henry, her life would have been a lot better.

At first Flourish couldn't help her but wonder how Henry managed to get a job at the oil company. But the hidden misery behind him getting that job was his sister.

Benedetto, his sister used to be a member of the oil managers, but when she became pregnant, she was given a maternity leave that involved a year and six months.

She just couldn't leave her brother to wander off like a lost sheep; she had to help him so that was how he got the job.

"You are shocked aren't you''. Henry said smiling.

"I'm not shocked because I know that you did not use your brain to get this job and anyway why do you keep on disturbing me, just leave me alone.'' She said as she took her bucket and mop and left.

After finishing her work, she went home. She didn't know that her uncle had planned something for her. When she got home, everyone was smiling, the children, flora, and even SULE her uncle was also smiling. She began to wonder what was going on that was making everybody smile at her.

"Ah, am I safe, this one that you all are smiling at me that way.'' She asked coldly.

"We are all smiling because we have good news for you, news that would blow your mind'' Flora said as she gently tapped her back. JOY began to wonder what the news was all about.

"Could it be they have found a new job for me.'' She thought to herself.

"Now what have you all planned for me?'' she said smiling and blushing at the same time. "Well you know that my friend, Thomas.'' He asked dramatically.

"Yes, I remember him, what has happened." She replied.

"He has a son named jerry. My friend told me that his son likes you and that he would have loved to meet you and get to know you more" he said still happy.

"So?" Asked Flourish who couldn't figure out what was making her uncle so happy.

"What kind of question is that, can't you see that I'm trying to hook you up with somebody that really cares about you and not that man you call your husband who doesn't really care about you?" He replied angrily. He couldn't believe that all his niece could say was "so?"

"But uncle, I don't want an arranged marriage and by the way I'm still married to my husband"

"Husband my foot. A man that does not care about you shouldn't be given that title. He does not even deserve to be called a man talk less of even a mere husband." He said angrily as he left the sitting room. He was already overwhelmed with a lot of anger burning inside of him.

Flourish just fell to the ground. It was as if her world had come crashing down. She loved her husband so much. He met the whole world to her but what did he do? He abandoned her just because she couldn't bear a child for him. Is that what love for a partner is supposed to be?

During their wedding to each other they had each promised each other that they would be together no matter the circumstances that may occur whether they are facing hardships or what have you.

But look at what had happened. Flora could understand what was going on in flourish mind. It wasn't easy for a woman to just let go like that.

"I can understand what you are going through, but you and I both know that your husband is probably getting married to some other woman so why not just move on with your life." Flora said trying to make her change her mind. It was really important that she moved on with her life.

"Who would want to marry a barren woman like me? Eh, tell me. No man would want to look at my direction because I won't be able to bear children for him, so it makes no difference of me going out to look for another man." She said still sobbing. She was feeling too weak to even do anything.

"Don't curse yourself. You are not a barren woman, you should know by now that both me and your uncle don't see you that way." She said trying to console her.

Flourish decided that it was about that time she let go of the past and focus on what the future holds for her. It is said that we don't usually know what the future has in stored for us, but we just have to work towards seeing a brighter future for ourselves.

The next day when she got to work, she was sacked. The manager had summoned her to his office only to give her a sack letter.

"But sir what have I done to receive this sack letter." Flourish asked in tears. She just couldn't believe what she was seeing. "Madam, one of my clients reported that you were trying to sexually harass him despite knowing that he is a married man. You are not worthy of staying here because our clients are not safe." The manager said.

"Madam please just go." The manager said pointing towards the direction of the door. Flourish had no choice but to go. She knew who was behind all that happened but just kept quiet. She wasn't really happy with the job so she found it a pleasure leaving it.

On her way outside she bumped into a woman. The woman appeared to be harsh, so before anything happens Flourish decided to apologize.

"Oh sorry ma I wasn't watching where I was going." Flourish said as she continued her journey but was drawn back by a devilish woman ready to unleash her evil wrath.

"Do you think you can just say sorry and go scot free?" The woman said like those evil step mother's in the olden days

Flourish knew she was doomed. She didn't understand why the woman was after her. She wondered if her village people have finally decided to kill her.

The woman seeing that Flourish was already getting frightened by the way she was talking decided to talk in a more polite and friendly way.

"My dear you seem stressed, what's the problem." The woman asked pretentiously. Flourish found it strange talking to a stranger she barely even knew.

"Ma, I don't know you so it will be stupid of me to share my problems with you. I mean I don't see any reason why I should be telling you what's going on in my mind." She replied sharply.

"It is said that you shouldn't walk out on your elders, I may be sent by God to solve your problems." Hearing that Flourish had a change of thought. She decided to tell the strange woman what was going on in her mind. She didn't know that day was going to begin her days of woe.

"Ma, let's go somewhere to talk. I don't want to stay here even for a second." Flourish said trying to look for a place to go.

The woman had a car, so she took this to her advantage. "I brought a car so we can perhaps go there and discuss." Flourish still didn't know what was making her talk to someone she didn't know. Maybe it was because she was a woman so she had so much trust on her. They both went to where the woman packed her car to discuss.

"Well before we start discussing, my name is Jane." The woman said introducing herself as she requested for a handshake.

"My name is Flourish." She said shaking her.

"So what's your problem? Are you perhaps looking for a job or what?" The woman asked looking so interested.

“Ma, it’s as if you just knew my problem. I started working here yesterday, but the enemies still don’t want me to work here, today I came to work only to get a sack letter claiming I did something I had no idea of. Now I don’t know where to go and start working.” Flourish said staring at the woman who was just laughing at her sad pathetic story. This made Flourish a little bit annoyed.

“Now why are you laughing, is there anything funny in what I said?” Flourish said a little bit upset.

“Hmm, my child, I told you that God had sent me to solve your problem, I have a brother who has a company at Abuja, that company pays him a lot of money. He is actually looking for some workers; he told me that he pays his clients good amount of money so none of his clients suffer financial crises.” The woman said lying.

“Really madam so what am I waiting for?” Flourish said really so excited. “I don’t think so, you will have to do something first.” She said facing downwards.

"But what could that be?" Flourish asked very furious.

"My brother wants a wife , I told him that I will look for a woman, he had complained to me so many times that he does not want an arranged marriage, so I told him that I would bring a girl and if the both of them like each other then they can get married, I really want my brother to get married, see the job is yours but please get married to him, he is very sweet, cute and handsome, he is the dream of every woman; every woman wishes to spend a night with him." Jane said pleading.

Flourish had no idea what to do now. She also hated arranged marriages and she didn't even know if she was going to fall for him. She was thinking for over 3 minutes when Jane who was tired pinched her.

"What have you decided, if you still don't believe that he's handsome then here is his picture." Jane said showing her the photo. The guy was really handsome and cute. Flourish was already falling for him just by looking at his photo.

"Didn't I tell you, please just get married to him, whenever you are ready, I will take you to Abuja?" Flourish wasn't too sure if she should go with Jane but she had to give it a thought.

"No problem, I will think about it and give you feedback and anyway what about your number, you know I need to contact you."

"Oh yes, do you have your phone there, I want to call it." Jane gave Flourish her number and her address to keep in touch with her. Flourish was happy but was also feeling sober because of what had happened before she met the woman.

Her uncle noticed it and decided to talk to her. "My child what happened today, you don't seem so happy?" He asked sensing something was going on.

"I was sacked." She replied releasing the bullet.

"What?" Exclaimed her uncle who was shocked on hearing what she said. "You can't be serious. How could you have being sacked? I mean what did you do?" This made Flourish to feel sad.

Her uncle noticed this and went close to where she was and placed her head on his shoulder.

"My dear talk to me, don't feel bad. I'm here just tell me what happened." With this flourish felt relaxed and decided to open up to her uncle.

"Well uncle, when I went to work today, my manager summoned me to his office only to give me a sack letter. But thanks to God for bringing that woman to me." She said raising her hands up to glorify God.

"And which woman is that." Sole asked confused. "Well uncle, it's a long story, but I would be glad to share it with you, while I was coming out from the company, I bumped into a woman, she realized I was feeling sober and she asked me what was going on, she told me about her brother in Abuja who had a company that fetch a lot of money and that he was looking for some workers, she told me I already have the job but I will have to marry him." She said with a sense of relief.

"What, marry someone you don't know, I hope you didn't accept the offer." He said so angry.

"Uncle, this is not a matter of marriage, she is offering me a free job, I can't let this opportunity just slip off my hand and anyway the guy is really handsome, she showed me his picture." She said rest assured.

"My child, I doubt that woman, who knows she might be a trafficker." He said really concerned. He was scared because he didn't want anything bad to happen to his niece.

"Uncle there is nothing to be scared about, she is a woman and she is only being helpful and concerned about her fellow gender, and anyways you were the one who told me to find a guy and now I'm telling you that I like this guy so what's the big deal, why are you still objecting." She said wanting to stand up rudely but stopped.

"Hmm." Suleiman sighed. "Well anyways it's your choice. Who am I to stop you? But have you considered seeing him face to face." Flourish knew that her uncle would ask such a question.

"Uncle, the woman told me that if I'm ready, she will take me to Abuja to meet her brother, from the look of things; I think I'm ready to go, I have her number, I will call her." Flourish said bringing out her phone to call her.

"Hello who is this?" Jane asked not knowing who she was speaking with.

"It's me Flourish, the woman you met earlier today. The same woman that you promised to take to Abuja." Flourish said smiling. Her uncle just stood nodding his head. It seemed he already had the feeling that things were not going to end well.

"Oh, you should have said so at the beginning, so have you agreed." Jane asked eagerly.

"Yes I'm ready to meet him, I'll come to your house tomorrow and then we can go." Flourish said smiling. She was using one of her eyes to look at her uncle trying to see his reactions. It seemed he wasn't okay with the idea that she was going.

"Okay, then make sure you come early." She said and cut the call. She was so happy that Flourish had agreed. She quickly called her brother to inform him that his bride was on her way.

“My child it is well with you. I just hope and pray that you find that happiness you are desperately seeking for.” He said as he kissed her forehead and left the room.”

Meanwhile, Flourish was just thinking about how her wedding would be. She couldn’t wait to go to Abuja. She believed that if she goes there she would be able to start her life afresh. She started packing her bags ready to go but another thought came in to her mind. She thought that maybe she still won’t be able to bear a child for her new husband. She managed to drive the thought away and started thinking about him. On the other hand, there was a job and she needed that job badly. She was sure she would be free from henry and any other thing from her past but I guess she was wrong. She never knew that she going to Abuja would only cause a lot of problems. She also met her past again.

The next day, Flourish hurriedly left the house. She boarded a cab to Jane’s house. Jane had been eagerly waiting for her. She was getting impatient by the passing seconds.

"My sister thank God you are here. Do you know how long I've been waiting for you? Well anyways forget about that let's quickly go to the airport before we miss our flight." Jane said trying to hurry. Their flight was to be by 9:15am and it was already 8:45am. They were really running out of time, and neither Jane nor Flourish wanted to miss this opportunity.

They were able to make it to the airport in time for their flight. Early that morning Jane had asked her brother if he would be at home. While they were on the plane Jane told flourish that Joshua which was the name of her brother would be waiting for them at the airport.

Flourish was scared a little bit. She feared that maybe Joshua may not like her at first. All through the journey she was restless. She didn't even get the chance to view the world from up above. This was the first time she was entering a plane, and ever since she has been a little girl she had always told herself that when she does enter a plane for the first time, she would the world from up above. But due to her restlesness she didn't get the chance to do so.

In not less than an hour they had arrived in Abuja. "My brother should be here somewhere." Jane said looking all over the reception for her brother. Flourish turned to her left only to see a young handsome man waving towards her direction. She drew the attention of Jane who was curiously looking for him. "Is that your brother?" Asked flourish who sensed it could be him. Jane stretched her eyes and saw that was actually her brother. "Oh wow you could even recognize him from afar. Let's go." Jane said faking smiles.

Jane took Flourish to where Joshua was. Joshua already liked at first sight. Flourish has a natural beauty. Any sensible guy would fall in love with her at first sight.

"Hi." Joshua said shyly. "Hi." Flourish replied also feeling shy. She didn't know what next to say. She just kept her head facing downwards.

Joshua could sense that Flourish was shy. Jane quickly signaled Joshua to take Flourish home. She knew that if she allowed them chitchat for so long they may end up not leaving the airport, and she didn't want that to happen. She wanted to take the next available flight back to Ibadan after dropping Flourish off.

"What's your name?" Joshua asked politely like those young boys would ask their fellow girlfriends while wooing them.

"My name is Flourish, and I'm very qualified for this job, you don't have to worry about a thing." She said really furious. She didn't want to lose the job.

"Don't worry let's go home. You must be very exhausted from your journey." He said holding her hand and helping her with her luggage. Flourish felt loved by his actions.

Ever since Flourish had been with David, he had never once helped her with her luggage whenever she came back from travel. She could remember vividly the incident that had happened with her returning from Port Harcourt after visiting a specialist on her infertile case.

David didn't even bother to give her a hug or even help her with her luggage. That day was the worst day of her life. She was so happy to see that

Joshua was being so considerate towards her and that's all she wanted.

"Flourish, you do have a soft hand." Joshua said jokingly. This made flourish to blush. While she was in the car, she focused her eyes on Joshua. He was just too cute to be ignored.

Joshua finally took Flourish to his house. She was so amazed by the building; it was just too magnificent that she just imagined herself living in such a house.

"Well this is your house make yourself feel comfortable, my brother will take you to his work place and he will tell you what to do, as for me I'm going back to Ibadan." Jane said pointing towards the chair beside where Flourish was standing so as for her to sit.

The idea that Jane was going back to Ibadan disturbed Flourish she felt that since she brought her here she was supposed to stay with her for at least a week or two.

"But this is not right; you know I don't really know your brother that much so I really need you to stay here with me for some time." Flourish said pleading.

"I have to go, from the look of things my brother is already falling for you, you guys have to be left alone so that you can bond." Jane said as she hurriedly left the house. She knew that Flourish was going to ask so many questions. So to avoid such questions she had to leave immediately.
"Where has my sister gone now?" Joshua asked. At first flourish did feel shy, but she came to like him.

CHAPTER 4

Joshua and flourish had started having feelings for each other, sometimes they would go for shopping together; go for night dinners and also to watch a movie.

Jane had told Joshua so many times to propose to flourish. She just wanted the both of them to get married immediately. She was ready to do anything possible to make the marriage happen.

Flourish was given a well-paid job at her fiancé's company. At work she was treated as a queen because to her clients she was like the second in command.

Sometimes Joshua would leave Flourish in charge of some of his big time transactions. At first, Flourish couldn't wait anymore for when she would finally have a new engagement ring on her fingers but changed her mind when she realized a slight change in her fiancé's behavior.

She never knew him to be a hard time alcoholic; maybe Jane intentionally didn't want her to be aware about her brother's bad side. She is expected to at least let the girl she wants as her brother's life partner to be aware about her brother's character.

"Baby, I don't like the fact that you drink too much, I mean it's not healthy for you." Flourish had said while trying to serve lunch for her babe. They had just returned from their tiring day's job.

Joshua didn't like the facts that flourish had the guts to say something like that. He got annoyed but didn't want to throw it on her. He didn't want to ruin the plan that both him and his sister had managed to cook up.

He then decided that it was about that time he proposed to her and eventually gets married to her. He wanted to get intimate with her but he realized that whenever he tried coming close to her, she always rejected and pushed him away telling him to wait till they were married.

She was no virgin at all so it was useless trying to wait till marriage. She knew how she used to boast to her friends before she met the destroyer of her life on how she will keep herself till she's married. But I guess she just couldn't keep herself.

A month and 3 weeks had passed since both Joshua and Flourish had been together and living in the same house so Joshua decided to break the ice.

On one faithful evening, when flourish came home exhausted, Joshua arranged for a romantic evening dinner. He wanted to surprise her that day, by proposing to her.

He decorated the table with candles, a bottle of Eva wine was at the center of the table with glass at the opposite direction. The table was covered with red clothing and there was a design on the table that states. "Will you marry me?"

There were roses sprinkled on the table and the atmosphere was filled with love.

Flourish couldn't believe her eyes; no one had ever done such a sweet thing to her before. She was really amazed. “Is my dream finally coming true?” She thought to herself.

Right from where she was at the door step, she just couldn’t wait for when he would come and take her inside. True to her dreams, he went close to her, held her hand and took her to the table.

He helped her sit down and opened the wine. He poured it into both glasses and gave one to flourish. Flourish began to feel more and shyer as she realized her beloved was staring at her. Their eyes met and flourish began to blush.

Flourish couldn’t believe that her dreams were coming true. Before she knew it, Joshua brought out a small box out of his breast pocket. Flourish wanted to start crying but she managed to hold it.

Joshua knelt down, looked into her eyes, opened the box and brought out a ring. This was the first time he was proposing to any woman. Though he was a natural flirt he had never once proposed to any woman he had come in close contact with.

He had bought a book of poetry. He didn't know the word to say to her that would make her giggle. He wanted something romantic and so one of his close friends suggested that he bought a book of poetry. He used his weekend to master all the key words in them.

"Roses are red. There is no one as beautiful as you. There is a saying that love at first sight is true love indeed. Yes, you are the love of my life and I'm not too sure if I would be able to live without you. Please Flourish will you marry me." He said smiling and taking the ring close to her fingers. Flourish couldn't express how happy she was; she turned her face to the other side and smiled, then she looked at Joshua. He was a handsome guy, and no girl in her right senses would want to refuse such a great opportunity.

After about 2 minutes of silence, Flourish finally agreed. With her tiny sweet voice, she said. "Yes I will marry you." With that Joshua didn't hesitate to place the ring on her finger. He did that and gave her a kiss. All the while they've been living together in the same house they have never one day kissed each other.

It was a dream come true to Flourish. Joshua later spoon fed her; he promised her that he was going to make their wedding a grand one. Flourish then called flora to tell her that she had already been engaged.

She knew her aunt was going to be so excited to hear the fact that she was engaged. As far as she knew, moving on with her life was the most important aspect of her life. She couldn't just stay stagnant waiting for the period when David would come begging.

Jane was finally happy. She couldn't wait anymore for the wedding. She told herself that she was going to specifically place the arrangements of the wedding on her head.

No one wanted to take chances, especially flourish who just wanted to get married to Joshua by all mist.

She didn't want to lose this opportunity she had to finally move on with her life. Sometimes moving on isn't that easy. In Flourish's case, she still kept on pondering on the issue of her not bearing a child. Every time she thinks of it, she tries shunning it away but it still won't leave. It wouldn't be more than a year after her wedding with Joshua that the truth would be revealed. She was just too scared. Well on her wedding day, she had a talk with Flora.

It was as if Flora knew what was on her mind. While she was being dressed for her big day, Flora walked into her room. She wanted to speak to her. Every mother would want to give her child some piece of advice on the day of her wedding. And to Flora, Flourish was still her daughter.

"Hi." Flora said smiling. She was so happy seeing how beautiful her niece was. She was being applied make up.

"Oh aunt you don't know how happy I am to see you here. Please just give me a hug." She said opening her hands wide enough to receive her aunt.

"Hmm, it makes me so happy to see you happy, but I can see that you are sad inside of you. I know why you are sad and that is why I'm here to speak to you." Flora said concerned.

Flourish knew where she was driving at but didn't want to talk about it. "Aunt please let's not bother talking about it. Today's a happy day for me; I don't want you ruining it." She said facing the other side.

All of a sudden, she became so rude to the makeup artist. "Can't you do your job properly, you almost blinded my eyes." She said rudely even though that wasn't what happened. But the artist tolerated her and continued with her job.

"Why are you pouring out your anger on this girl? See I don't want you to ruin your life by spending all day thinking about the fact that you are infertile. There is a saying that you shouldn't start your day with the broken pieces of yesterday, you should begin your day with happiness and never the less fill your heart with positive things so that your day would be……"

"Aunt I don't get it. What are all these proverbs you are cooking up for me? I really do not understand anything." She said interrupting her aunt and in a tone of absolute disgust.

"All I'm trying to say is don't start this new marriage with the problems from your former marriage. Try to start all over again. When you do get married, don't always be feeling moody so that your husband doesn't feel suspicious of your problems. Who knows he might never come to know about it." She said feeling confident about what she said.

"Oh thank you aunt, I'm so thankful for this advice you have given me. You just gave me a relief from all the problems." She said putting her hands together. She never knew that her problems were just about to begin.

After their wedding, that was a week after, Joshua started showing his other behavior. It was as if he had lost so much interest in Flourish.

He comes home very late at night, on one occasion when he came home, he was drunk. Flourish managed to take him up to his room. As she was trying to take his clothes off she saw some used condoms. Tears began to flow down her cheeks.

She said within herself that she had not even had a memorable intimate relationship with her husband but yet he was already cheating. “Could it be that I’m not satisfying him that’s why he went outside. No... No I can’t just jump into conclusion; I will have to interrogate him first.” She said feeling insecure. She lay down beside her husband. She just could not believe that she was been cheated on. Throughout the whole night, she kept on thinking. She didn’t know how to express herself to him but she eventually slept off.

When it was morning she didn’t wait for Joshua to get up, she just went and poured cold water on him.

“What…what happened.” Joshua shouted.

“Where were you last night?” Flourish asked in anger as she brought out the used condom. She was disgusted at the sight of it but had to hold on to it.

“I was at work, where else would I be?” He replied unaware of what was going on, as he opened his eyes after a long day of sleep.

"Your girlfriend's house I guess." Flourish said really angry.

"What are you saying? I was at work." "You were at work, then why did I see this used condom in your trouser? We have not really had a nice intimate relationship together and you are already cheating." She said wanting to cry.

Joshua didn't know what pit he was digging himself into. He shouldn't have gotten married to flourish. To him she wasn't given him that much satisfaction he deserved, especially the satisfaction one gets from intimacy.

Some say marriages are sweet, but then after sometime they get tired of the relationship. They had not even gone for their honeymoon and they were already having problems. Flourish began to see that it was a bad idea of her getting married to Joshua.

Joshua drew himself closer to flourish and placed his hand on her shoulder which she took off immediately. "Get your stinky hand away from my shoulder, you disgusting man." She said eyeing him. That word disgusting made Joshua angry that he almost slapped but he withdrew himself. He didn't want to do anything bad out of anger.

"Do you want a honeymoon, I've already started planning our honeymoon to Dubai and you were already misinterpreting me. Is that how couples behave to each other? He said winking his eyes. Aren't they supposed to trust each other?"

It seems that flourish wasn't so dull after all. She didn't even believe or paid any attention to what he said. "So you think you can deceive me, you think I will fall for this ridiculous badly scripted impocrisy. You are cheating on me and you want us to go for our honeymoon at Dubai, what's the use now."

Joshua didn't know what to do next; he was finding it hard coping with flourish. He didn't say anything again; he just went to his wardrobe and stared at her. She just sat like an old woman. Her legs were wide open like those busy bodied women who like gossip. Her hair was looking so untidy; she looked like a mad woman.

Joshua was looking at the figure he got married to. At first he didn't know what aspect of her body he fell in love with.

"Darling, just pack your bags. We are going to Dubai." He said as he went to take his bath. He smelled badly.

They went to Dubai. To Flourish it was a honeymoon filled with love, but to Joshua it was a honey moon filled with torture. He didn't enjoy his stay at Dubai despite they visited so many tourist centers.

On one occasion when they visited one tourist center they bumped into an old friend of Flourish. It was Bella's boyfriend, Travis.

"Oh wow, we bumped into each other, so how is Henry." Travis asked unaware of what transpired between the both of them. He was never told of what happened.

"Oh hi Travis." She said scared that maybe he may reveal her secret. She was just so short of words.

"Flourish who is this guy." Joshua asked suspecting something was wrong. He was really good at suspecting.

"Am...Am he was my old friend." Flourish said really scared. She was just sweating. Travis didn't know what was going on he just decided to ask of the pregnancy.

"How is your baby?"

"Which baby?" Flourish asked panicking. She didn't know why Travis had to come at that moment. She was trying so hard to signal Travis to stop talking. "Anyway this is my husband, Joshua." She said hoping that would change the way Travis was speaking.

Joshua still didn't understand what the guy meant by baby. It was too complicated and he decided to ask when they got to the hotel. All he knew was that something fishy was going on.

"Well Travis I will talk to you later." Flourish said as she quickly took Joshua away from the scene. She didn't want any of her secrets to be exposed.

On getting to the hotel, Joshua decided to ask her who Travis was. "Flourish who was that guy? And why was he talking about some kind of baby?" He said taking off his shoes.

To flourish that question was a bomb in her ears; she didn't know how to answer the question. "His name is Travis and we were best of friends while we were at school." She said stammering as she faced the other side. Her heart was beating faster than ever. It was as if she was about to have a heart attack.

Joshua knew that something wasn't right. He decided to ask another bombastic question.

"Then why was he asking about Henry? And you still haven't answered my previous question. Which baby was he talking about?"

"Well…well…" Flourish said stammering. Joshua had finally caught his fish in his bait. He could understand all that was going on just by her silence.

"No need to answer that question, we all has past life, anyways we are going back to Nigeria tomorrow so start packing, I'm going to have some barbecued fish, if you want some you can join." He said faking smiles.

Flourish was happy; she thought that maybe he didn't care. She agreed to join him in eating the barbecued fish.

The next day they both went to the airport to take their flight back to Nigeria.

After they had come back to Nigeria their worries began and their marriage was beginning to crash.

Joshua and Flourish had been trying their very best to have a child but it seems that flourish infertility had come back haunting her. Joshua found no use sleeping with her because he knew that no matter what he does she still won't be able to bear a child for him.

He started womanizing, sleeping with different types of women. As God would have it, Joshua came home very late at night, he was also very drunk, and this time Flourish refused to take him to his room instead she started raining abuses at him. This made Joshua so angry that he threw it out on her.

He started beating her up and said to her. "You infertile woman, you can't give me a child, instead of you to go to a hospital and treat yourself you are here talking back at me, you are such a shameless woman." He continued hitting her which eventually led to an injury.

Flourish was pleading for him to stop but Joshua didn't stop. He was so upset and angry that he had to say what he never wanted to say.

"If you don't know, know now that I'm already a father to 3 kids and I'm expecting a fourth." Flourish was tongue tied after hearing those words. Her husband already had 3 children outside their marriage and he was even expecting a fourth. While she couldn't even give her husband just one child.

The pain she was receiving from the beating was not compared to the pain of not having children. She started blaming nature for not being too good to her.

The next day, she called Flora to tell her about the pains she was going through in Joshua's house, how he keeps on making fun of her and tells her he has children outside marriage.

While on the phone Flora felt the pain in flourish's words. Nothing would pain a woman more than when she is unable to bear a child. Flourish had made a mistake in the past and now it was now avenging her.

Flora had nothing else to say, the only thing she could say to Flourish were some words of comfort. At least at the moment Flourish needed those words. By then, Joshua had stopped flourish from working. She was now a regular housewife. Her job was now to take care of the house chores.

She would wake up very early in the morning to prepare breakfast for her husband before he goes to work. She would have to wash the dishes, clean the house and even wash his car. Before they married, they had someone doing for them, but because of the problems they now have Joshua had to sack all those workers so that Flourish could do the entire job. Flourish had barely spent six months with Joshua.

This pained Flourish a lot; she had no choice but to call Jane who introduced her into this mischievous business.

Jane who heard her brother already had children outside told him to start getting things ready to bring the woman and her children into the house. She didn't want her brother to live with a woman who could not bear a child for him. So when Flourish called her she knew the reason already.

Jane got to the house only to see Flourish crying. "Ah what happened why are you crying?" Jane asked acting surprised like she knew nothing at all.

"Why won't I cry, when my husband does not love me again? He has children outside and he keeps on treating me like a complete stranger." Flourish said still crying. The pain was becoming unbearable for her.

Jane was feeling disgusted by the tears shed by Flourish. "Look dear, love is for teenagers. When it comes to marriage love is not involved, you just have to give your partner a child. See children are the pride of a man, a man without a child is seen as a worthless man whose manhood has been worn out. That is the reason why he had to go outside to have children seeing that you couldn't give him one." She said so selfishly.

How can a woman be so heartless towards her own fellow woman, it's really terrible that women can't even be each other's keeper.

"At least you are his sister you were the one who introduced me to him so you should be there to support me." Flourish said looking into her eyes.

"Hmm." Jane sighed heavily as she got up from the chair. "That's where you are getting it wrong, my brother is the only son of my father, it would be somehow if he does not have a child of his own, and anyways he always listen to me, he came to me and told me that you were unable to bear a child for him and that he has found a girl who already has three children and is expecting a fourth, I told him to treat those children well because they were his and I also told him to take good care of you." She lied.

“So you were supporting your brother all through.” Flourish said a little bit angry.

“Of course, if you were in my position won’t you have done the exact same thing I did, I didn’t want to disappoint my brother.” Jane said trying to look sober. She was tired of Flourish; she only regretted ever bringing Flourish into Joshua’s life.

In a way flourish felt Jane was right. No sister would want her brother to be childless. If they find out that he has a child outside his matrimonial home they would do everything in their power to bring those children in even though it involves sending away his wife.

Flourish knew it was all over. There was no hope for her in her husband’s house. “Look flourish all hope isn’t lost, go and see a doctor, I’m sure you will find a cure.” Jane said holding flourish hand pretending to pity for her.

“Look I’m going to be staying for the meantime so the both of us can find a date to see a doctor. Flourish didn’t know what to say. She knew there was no hope for her anymore.

The same thing that happened to her while she was with David was also repeating itself now that she was with Joshua. She knew Jane wasn't on her side anymore. Now that her brother has children outside she would do anything to drive her and bring those children in.

Flourish had no choice but to accept the fate in which nature had given to her. She had succeeded in ruining her life by herself.

That same day when Joshua returned home, he behaved so normal. He didn't get drunk as usual. Flourish didn't even bother to welcome him; instead she just sat on her bed reading a book titled "Marriages that never work." Joshua was annoyed at the sight of the book. He started talking and boasting about his children.

"I have reaped the fruit of my labour, now I'm blessed with a son and I will make sure I bring those children into this house." He said as he looked at Flourish that showed little or no interest in whatever he was saying.

She was just thinking about her life. Now she was certain she had gotten herself into a big mess.

At first she felt Joshua was a nice guy who was going to love her all his life but I guess she thought wrong.

There is a saying that goes do what you can do and leave the rest for God. That was exactly what she did. She had done all she could ever do but everything had paid for so she had to leave the rest for God. All she prayed was for Joshua not to bring his outside family into their matrimonial home. She got tired after all and eventually slept off.

Chapter 5

True to his words, Joshua actually brought Jacinta and the children to his house. Jane was super excited at the sight of the children as she rushed to hug them one after the other.

Flourish was at the kitchen cooking when she overheard some voices at the sitting room only to see some children and a pregnant lady. Tears began to run down her cheeks. Her worst nightmare had finally turned into a reality.

Before she could turn and go back to the kitchen, Jane immediately called her.
"Eh…Flourish you see these are Joshua's children please help them carry their luggage to the guest room and also, give them something to eat." Jane said addressing her as if she was like a housemaid. Well that was what Joshua had painted her to be.

What could poor Flourish have done? She had no choice but to behave as a house maid because she is treated as one.

"Come children, I will take you to your room." She said taking the three children to the guest room. They were really beautiful children but there was no sign of resemblance of the children to Joshua.

After she had taken the kids to the guest room she quickly went to prepare food for them, she didn't want Joshua to hit her for any reason, not when his other woman is around.

After she had taken care of that, she met Joshua and Jacinta sitting on one of the cushion chairs. She became jealous at the sight of seeing them together. She had never really been that close to Joshua and so it was just irr in her body. She decided to go back to her room. She didn't want to witness the love they were busy playing. But then Joshua stopped her only to make fun of her.

"Don't go there because that is not your room." He said laughing. Jacinta also joined him to laugh. Jane couldn't stop herself from laughing. This made Flourish really embarrassed.

"Why shouldn't I go there, isn't that my matrimonial home?" On hearing that, they all burst into a loud laughter.

"Matrimonial home, who dash you, see that room is for my baby here, Jacinta, she would be staying there with me so you better go and pack your belongings away from there and go live with the children in the guest room." He said with anger.

Flourish's life had been shattered into pieces. She had now become a house girl. Even though she was married, her husband doesn't even treat her well. She didn't even know the last time she had a kiss from Joshua. She had no other choice but to start packing. As she turned back to go upstairs Joshua called her back.

"And anyways I'm taking Jacinta to Canada, we want the child to be born there and then we would come back. we will be leaving by tomorrow." He said with a little grip. He had been finding it really hard to say those words.

"Please take care of my children; I know that you don't have children of your own so don't use this opportunity to maltreat my children." Jacinta said eyeing Flourish.

Flourish was been treated as a slave in Joshua's house. She was the one who arranged the kid's bedroom after they were done littering it. She was also the one who cooked for them and even packed their plates after they were done eating. When Jacinta and Joshua left, the kid's became even more arrogant and disrespectful.

Jacinta and Joshua spoilt the children so much that at their young age they already had phones.

The first child who was a girl was 10, the second was 6 and the third who was a boy was 4. The first girl was so disrespectful that she doesn't even listen to anyone.

On one occasion, Flourish told her to pack her plate but she refused saying. "Isn't that your job, house help?" That word made Flourish so angry that she took the stick for turning pap to hit her and she sustained some minor injuries.

What Flourish did to Precious cautioned others to learn a big lesson. At that time Jane had already gone back to Ibadan so it was just her and the children.

In no time flourish and the kid's began to know and understand each other. They now knew what flourish liked and disliked. This was as a result of the way Flourish disciplined them. Whenever they did something bad she would always flogged them. To avoid her beatings they always tried to do what was right.

Even precious didn't have to think twice before she knew she had to pack her plates. Flourish had noticed that the children had no resemblance to Joshua. She knew that if the children were his, they would look like him but none of them looked like him.

She didn't want to involve herself in Joshua's life so she decided to mind her business.

Three months later, Jacinta and Joshua came back home with another bouncing baby boy. This was double the joy for Joshua because he was blessed with yet another son. But on the other hand it was double the pain for Jacinta. The children weren't his. They were for one of her course mates back then at school and now he had come back looking for the children.

One day when she was taking some morning exercise she had encountered him. She realized he was coming towards her direction. She wanted to run away because she didn't want Joshua to see her with John.

But you know the saying, many days for the thief, one day for the owner. How long could she run? She would get caught at the end. She decided to answer whatever question he may ask her.

"Ah Jacinta it's good I saw you." He said breathing so fast as a result of running after her.

"So what happened?" Jacinta said very angry. He was acting as if he had not seen her in about 30 years.

"I don't think I can do it anymore, I want my children." He said politely.

"Whose children, remember we made a deal." Jacinta said quickly in fears.

"I know we made a deal but my sister told me to come and take my children." With this Jacinta began to laugh and clapping her hands in the process.

"Look at this fool. It seems you have forgotten the deal we made, but don't worry, I will remind you. I told you that I will pay you money if you agree to sleep with me but I don't think I owe you or do I still owe you?" She asked out of fear. She was just looking at John's face. The kids did resemble him.

"At least let me see the children, let me see the baby just once and I promise I will go." John said pleading.

"Look I've told you so many times, please just go I don't want Joshua to come and see me here with you." She said looking round.

"But you and I know that you are unfair to the poor children, at least let them see their father, let me hug them and kiss their forehead, let me…."

"Enough, I've had enough, its better you just go, I don't want any problem." Jacinta said really angry. She only regretted ever having a deal with John.

"If only I knew something like this would happen I would never have a deal with you." She said eyeing him. John knew that he could not see his children anymore, he had tried all he could but Jacinta won't give in easily. So He went home hopelessly.

Jacinta didn't show any sign of pity for John, she didn't care about the real fatherly love she was depriving her children of; instead she just kept on raining abuses on him.

When she got home, she started thinking about how she met john and how she had to beg him to sleep with her.

Some years back, she fell in love with Joshua, they did things together and at that moment she was a final year student. Because of how poor she was, he sponsored her education to final year. Their love continued to blossom. She knew that the only way to continue to enjoy his money was if she was able to bear a child for him. She knew that Joshua was not the type of guy that would reject her if she came to him pregnant.

But she had tried so many times to get pregnant by Joshua but it seems all efforts were in vain. She even slept with Joshua when she was ovulating but she still wasn't able to get pregnant.

She feared that she could be infertile and so she went to see a doctor who told her nothing was wrong with her. She then realized that it was Joshua who had the problem.

She then decided to meet her friend, Tami tope. Tope had a boyfriend and so when she met Jacinta she wanted to set up with a guy but Jacinta dammed the idea saying she wants to be a virgin all her life.

So when Jacinta came to tell Tope about her problem, Tope laughed. "I thought you were not interested." Tope said as she laughed.

"Why are you doing like this I'm telling you I have a serious problem at my hand and you are there laughing. What's your problem self." Jacinta said really angry.

"A beg no go chop me raw, no vex, a beg repeat your problem." Tope said making fun of her.

"See this my guy eh, he used to spend on me and I know that the only way to continue and enjoy his money is to have a child for him but I've been trying my very best to get pregnant by him, I even sleep with him when I'm on my ovulation but yet I still can't get pregnant, I even went to see a doctor who told me that there was nothing wrong with me." Jacinta said a little bit worried.

"See Jacinta, there is no problem with this; I've seen a lot of stories like this and I've also seen the solutions to this problems. See look for a very fertile guy, crack a deal with him, tell him to sleep with you and that you will pay him a huge amount of money, when you've gotten pregnant by him, tell your precious guy that you are pregnant and he would think he has impregnated you, it's that easy."

At that moment Jacinta was tongue tied. She had such an easy means yet she was cracking her brains. She still had one problem to tackle. She didn't know which guy to meet.

After some close thoughts she then decided to go after a first year student. It was then she met John, a quiet and good looking guy. She found out that he was in desperate need of money so it would be perfect to make the deal with him.

She paid John a hundred and eighty thousand when she got pregnant for her first child. She would collect money from Joshua and sometimes steal to pay john.

As for Jacinta, She was scared. She was just moving from one place to another, Flourish caught sight of this and decided to check her out.

"By the way, I've noticed something in the children, they don't actually look like Joshua, I'm afraid they are not his." She said like a detective asking a criminal some questions.

"Don't say that, they are his children" Jacinta said stammering.

"Did I ever mention they are not his children, but you and I both know they are not his children? If I want I would tell him but I'm not that wicked like you. I tend to consider others" Flourish said winking at her. "Well you are just a slave here so you have no right to interfere in my life?"

That word slave made Flourish very angry that she slapped Jacinta. "I'm not a slave, I'm the wife of Joshua, that I do all the chore in this house doesn't means I'm a slave! So you have no right to call me that" Flourish said pointing her finger at her.

This made Jacinta so angry that she retaliated. They started fighting and this caught the attention of Joshua who came downstairs to try and separate them.

"What is happening here, Flourish I hope you have not forgotten your place" Joshua said very angry as he faced her.

"So am I to blame for what this stupid goat has done?" Flourish said, pointing at Jacinta.

"Hey, you better watch your mouth" Jacinta said wanting to fight. Before they could do anything else they all heard a knock at the door. Flourish rushed to open the door and to Jacinta's surprise it was her long lost enemy, John.

"How can I help you?" Flourish asked because she didn't know him. "I want to see Joshua." John said as he looked round for Joshua.

Joshua didn't know who the guy was. Flourish allowed him to come in. Right there where Jacinta was, she was sweating. She knew that the only reason why he must have come here was to take his children.

"Hello, do I know you?" Joshua asked.

"No you don't, but Jacinta here does." Joshua at first didn't understood what he was saying, but he knew he had to pay homage. "At least let me get you some water." Joshua said trying to be friendly. "No, there is no need for that; I came here for serious business."

Joshua became scared when he heard serious business. "See I'm here to take my kids." John said.

"I beg your pardon, which children are you talking about?" Joshua asked very annoyed this time. "See my brother, the children you think are yours are actually mine." That word made Joshua so angry that he asked john to leave his house.

"Who are you to question the father of my children? Please leave my house?" Joshua said really angry as he pointed towards the direction of the door. "My brother you won't believe me when I say that I had a deal with your wife, Jacinta."

"I'm not interested in what deal you cracked in the past but please just leave my house"

John was still not ready to give in. He was going to make sure he revealed the secrets Jacinta had been hiding for a long time now, and most of all, take back his kids.

The only reason why he came back for his children was because he was unfortunate. He had lost both his wife and his two beautiful children in a fire outbreak. It all happened that while both his wife and kids were at their mum's shop, the little girl mistakenly spilled some of the fuel that their mum had bought. Unknowingly to the poor woman, who was about to turn on the stove close to where the fuel was spilled, also mistakenly lighted the matches and threw it on the spilled fuel, and then boom. There was a large explosion. There was also light and so the fire spread really fast. Before help could come, their body had been completely burnt. John mourned their death for a very long time before he remembered that he had other children, he knew he would have to go get them. So he wasn't going to stop now and lose hope.

Chapter 6

Joshua wasn't ready to believe that John was telling the truth. "So what deal did the both of you crack?" Joshua asked John.

"I was just a new student when Jacinta came to me; she told me she wants a child for her guy but she found out that he was infertile, she told me that she will pay me a huge amount of money if I agree to impregnate her and at that time I was in desperate need of money. I had no choice but to accept the offer, we've been doing this for all the children, I told her that I will never come to take the children but I had no choice because I lost my wife and children." Joshua was speechless after hearing the whole story.

So he was actually infertile. Jacinta was confused. "Is what this guy saying the truth." Joshua asked very angry as he headed towards her in a fit of rage.

"Well…well he's lying, I don't even know him; don't believe a word he tells you." Jacinta said stammering. She didn't know that John came prepared.

"If I'm lying then let's have a DNA test on the children and see who their father really is." John said in confidence that they were his children. Joshua was scared; he didn't want the children to turn out to be John's.

While in the hospital, Joshua was scared, he was just panicking about the identity of the children. Jacinta on the other hand was sweating. Her heart was beating faster than before. John was not scared at all, he knew the children were actually his. When the doctor came out, Jacinta began to panic. "The children's DNA doesn't match with that of Mr. Joshua but they do match with that of Mr. John. So I'm afraid to say that Mr. John is the biological father of the children." Those words were thunderous in Joshua's head.

He had nothing that he wanted to do to Jacinta. He just told her to pack her belongings and take the children away. Flourish couldn't stay in the house again, she planned to go back to Daniel but then she remembered he was already married.

She had no choice but to go back to Ibadan and stay with her uncle. While packing her luggage, Joshua tried to stop her. He was pleading with her to stay but she refused.

"Please Flourish I've learnt my lesson, now I realize how good you are, please don't go I still love you." He said as he knelt down pleading. He knew Flourish won't listen to him so he decided to call Jane. But Jane told him to let her go.

Flourish life experiences with Joshua had really taught her a lot of lessons. When she got back to Ibadan, her uncle hugged her. He was so excited to see her.

"Oh my child, you are welcome." He said.

"Uncle it wasn't easy at all." She said feeling frustrated.

"I know, but I warned you that the idea was too strange but you didn't listen, anyway enough of that. It's good you are here." He said as he rushed to the kitchen to get some juice. At last Flourish was finally free from the bondage that held her captive for so long.

After sometime she decided to go learn a trade. She told her uncle of the idea of learning tailoring. He agreed at once without a second thought. She started learning a trade and after sometime her uncle bought her a sewing machine. It also began to dawn in her to go back to David. She knew he must have had been married by now and probably have kids. She told her uncle about the idea but he objected to the idea.

"You know that David is married and yet you still want to go back?" He said like a reasonable father would talk to his daughter.

"I know he is married but he still hasn't divorced me yet." She said trying to make him understand. "Uncle you have done so much for me and I really appreciate, at least let me go and see him." Suleiman just wanted the best for his niece. He agreed and with the little money Flourish had, she went back to Lagos.

She didn't know that David wasn't a father yet. Joan and David had both been trying to have a child but they couldn't. It even got to a point that David began to think he was the one infertile but it was actually Joan.

She appeared to be good and innocent but inside she was a demon, a prostitute. While she was in her teens, she used to sleep with different boys. She sometimes used protection but one unlucky day for her she didn't use protection and she contacted a very deadly STI; syphilis. She didn't treat it on time thereby rendering her infertile. Since that incidence she started behaving innocently and that was what caught the attention of David's mother who just wanted Flourish out.

Whenever Joan would complain about her childless state, David's mother would always blame it on Flourish. I guess David's mother just had a natural hatred towards Flourish.

When Flourish eventually came, David welcomed her with all his heart. Despite being away from her he still loved her.

Joan on the other hand was really upset. She felt jealous because David spent much of his time with Flourish. One night she decided to talk to David.

"Honey, I still can't believe that you are still talking to that Flourish." She said in disgust. "Babe what are you saying, she is still my wife."

"Just hold it there, she is not your wife, don't you remember what mama said. She is the cause of our childlessness; she doesn't want us to have children." Jane said angrily.

"Do you believe everything that mama says, it is clear that mama doesn't like Flourish and that is why she is laying false accusations on her." David said holding firm to his word.

"See honey I'm not comfortable with Flourish staying here, she disgusts me; I have a feeling that's she's even using black magic to block my womb." Joan said at the top of her voice.

"What are you saying? I know that you don't like Flourish but that doesn't mean she is bad." He said tired. He knew that Joan won't stop talking so he decided to go to bed.

Joan on the other hand knew that it would be very hard convincing David to throw Flourish out of the house; she then decided to go see a prophetess.

Very early the next morning, Joan went to see her prophetess in a village far away. She didn't want anything galloping in her precious plan. She was ready to do anything to get Flourish out of her house.

When she got to the prophetess house, she was highly disgusted because the shrine lacked hygiene. “My daughter you are welcome.” The prophetess said as she saw that Joan wasn’t concentrating at all.

“Good morning my….my lady.” She stammered as she had no idea on how to address the prophetess. The prophetess on the other hand laughed and said. “Is that’s how you greet your mother at home, call me my prophetess, and what’s your problem.” The woman said.

“Sorry my prophetess but if I tell you my problem, you yourself would be very tired. I’m suffering so much in my marital life all because of my husband’s first wife.” The prophetess didn’t understand what she was saying but she knew she had to solve the problem.

“So my child what do you want me to do. Do you want me to kill her or what?” Joan liked the idea of killing flourish, but she wanted her to be maltreated.

“See my prophetess; I’m barren that is why I and my husband are unable to have a child. I’ve also noticed that he shows so much love towards his former wife and I really get jealous.

I've been trying my very best to blame our childless state on her, but my husband is not willing to believe, that is the main reason why I came here. I want you to come to my house and tell everybody that Flourish is the one to be blamed for my childless condition so that my husband would drive her away." Joan said.

"Hmm." The prophetess sighed. She knew that what Joan wanted her to do was wrong. "But my child don't you think that it is unfair to the poor girl, I mean what has she done wrong." The prophetess asked feeling pity for Flourish. "See my prophetess, money is not the problem, I will give you whatever amount of money you desire, but please just do what I ask of you" Joan said pleading. On hearing money the prophetess had a rethink. She decided to carry out the devilish plan.

"Please come tomorrow, I will give you my phone number and address." Joan said as she brought out a paper and pen from her purse. She wrote her number and address and gave it to the prophetess.

"Here is my number, so you can reach me, please don't disappoint me; I'm counting on you, if you are able to carry out this mission successfully, I will give you whatever amount you want."

Joan was ready to pay millions just to get Flourish out. Joan went home happy. Another problem she had was how to arrange for the money. She didn't consider that a problem again, she was able to sweet talk David into giving her the money.

The next day, she arranged for everyone to be at the sitting room. She was patiently waiting for the prophetess. David had no idea why Joan would summon them so early.

"Joan what is happening. Why have you asked us to wait here?" David asked surprised.

"Honey you don't seem to believe me when I tell you that Flourish is the cause of our childlessness that is why I have invited a prophetess, I called her yesterday to come today but I don't know where she is yet." Joan said looking outside the window.

"Joan you know I don't believe in all these superstitious belief and……" "I know but Flourish is the one to blame.' She quickly cut in.

After about 10 minutes of waiting, the prophetess finally arrived.

"Ah my prophetess!" Joan bowed. They all greeted and David became disgusted at the sight of the prophetess. "Joan who is this bush woman you've brought here?" He said angry.

"Honey please sit down, you have no right to call her bush woman and who knows she might be the key to our happiness. Flourish herself already knew that Joan was the compromise behind everything.

"My son, you might call me a bush woman or what have you, I really don't care all I know is that I come in peace. My daughter here called me to come to this house that she had something very important to tell me, so please what's the problem." She said beckoning on Joan.

By that time, Joan face had suddenly turned sober. "My prophetess, I and my husband are unable to bear a child, ever since this woman over here. [She said pointing towards flourish.] Came into our lives, she has been trying her very best to stop us from having kids." Joan said faking tears.

"Don't worry about that, but you know that it is not good to jump into conclusions just like that, I will have to talk to the gods whom I serve to find out if this woman is the cause of your childlessness." The prophetess said as she started incarnating. It was all part of their plan.

The noise became louder and louder and it annoyed David even more. "Hmm, this is bad; this girl is really a witch, from what the gods are telling me, she is the cause of your childlessness. She appears to be good looking and innocent but deep inside her she is a devil in disguise." The prophetess said nodding her head in pretense.

"So my doubt was true." Joan said facing David who had become so glued to the issue. David who had no interest in all these superstitious belief was now forced to believe. He couldn't believe that the Flourish he once loved was now betraying him. Flourish just stood at a distance and shook her head in self-pity. She applauded the drama well played by Joan.

"Flourish why did you do this?" David asked as some drop of tears flowed down his cheeks

"David, why would I do such a thing?" She said trying to explain herself but David was already blind folded by what the prophetess said. He started maltreating flourish. He made life unbearable for her. Joan on the other hand was super excited; she paid the prophetess a hundred thousand for a job well done.

Flourish had no reason staying there. She didn't know where she went wrong in her life that was making her go through all these crises.

She had been married to two men, and neither of them had been good to her for once. The one who she felt was her true lover actually left her, for a reason which she felt was too stupid to believe.

I mean, how can people who you barely even know, tell you evil things about your wife and you still would believe. Such a person could be described as a coward who can't bear to face reality.

Flourish at first wanted to go back to Ibadan, but she found it useless since her uncle had warned her but she failed to listen. Sometimes it is really important that we listen to the advice our elders tell us.

If only she had listened to him, then she wouldn’t have had to endure all that David was making her go through now. He treated her like her a slave in her own house, just as Joshua had did with her before.

She decided not to go back to Ibadan, so she just packed all her luggage and stood outside the gate like a beggar begging for alms.

Chapter 7

She sat on the bare floor hopeless; she had no house or anybody in Lagos that she wanted to stay with.

While she was sitting there, a guy in his car passed her. He reversed seeing how beautiful she was. He quickly drew the attention of flourish.

"What is a beautiful girl like you doing under this hot Sun?" The guy said smiling at

Flourish. He appeared to be very nice. Flourish didn't want anything to do with any man again. Her past life with Joshua had really taught her a great lesson.

"Please just leave me and let me be." Flourish said trying to drive him away.

Enoch was a pretty handsome guy; he was also a commissioner of the law. He worked hand in hand with the governor of Lagos. Governor Ague Solomon was a friend of Enoch while they were still at the university. The both of them were studying political science, but when they got to 300 levels. Enoch redrew and said he didn't want to study politics anymore. When they graduated, Solomon contested to be a governor of Lagos. To God be the glory, he won the election and became governor of Lagos.

Meanwhile Enoch had become a commissioner of the law. Solomon didn't want to offend his friend so he made him work hand in hand with him. The governor had cushioned him to get married but he refused saying. "We don't do things in a rush; I will find a nice girl to get married to." When Enoch saw Flourish, he considered her the right choice.

"See the sun is really hot, it will only darken your skin" Enoch said really concerned. "I have told you so many times that you should leave me, why don't you understand." Flourish said really angry. She didn't want anything to do with a man again.

"No problem I will go." Enoch said a disappointed. He left and vowed not to help her. But as God would have it. That very night when he was on patrol, he happened to meet her again at that same spot.

He couldn't just leave her and it was very late at night. Cultists were already hooding the whole area. He came down from his car and headed towards her.

"Madam it is not safe for you to be out here, cultists are already carrying out their activities." Enoch said again, this time really concerned.

"Please just leave me, let them kill me, I'm ready to die, nature hasn't been fair towards me." Flourish Said as some tears flowed down her cheeks. Enoch knew that if he didn't take her away from there sooner or later, she might lose her life.

The sounds of gun could be heard. Flourish couldn't even hear the sounds of gun shots; her life was too full of sorrow.

"Madam Gunshots are heard; please let me take you to a more secured environment." Flourish was getting scared as the gunshots increased. She decided to follow him and save her life.

She quickly put her luggage into the boots and entered into the car. Enoch drove her to a nearby inn within the environment. He had no relatives living around there and where he was living was quite far from where they were.

He took her to the inn and paid for at least 3 nights. He promised to come back the next day to at least talk to her. Flourish was happy; she finally had a place to lay her head.

She noticed that when the both of them were entering into the inn, a lot of people at the reception had their eyes fixed on the both of them. She knew what they would be thinking but she just ignored them. After some time, she finally went to bed.

Early the next morning after she had her bath, she heard a loud knock at the door. She thought it was the waiter, she had ordered some food to eat, but it was actually Enoch.

"Good morning Mr......" she said trying to recall his name.

"Mr. Enoch." He said in haste.

"Oh yes, please come inside." She said directing him into the room. Enoch sat on the bed while flourish sat on the only available chair. Before Flourish could say anything there was another knock on the door. Flourish suspected it was the waiter, so she took the food from his hands and placed on the table in between them.

It was their favorite. Fried rice.

"Well Mr. Enoch, I just want to say thank you, you've been too nice to me despite knowing I'm a stranger."

"Well it's by God divine grace; you won't believe that when I went to continue my patrol, I witnessed the killing of an innocent couple at the front of their house." Enoch said feeling down. It was such a painful sight. “What? Tell me what happened” flourish asked feeling pity for the couples.

“These couples were dressed in dinner dresses. It seemed they were going out for dinner. I was just driving and smiling at the couples when from nowhere they were shot. I was afraid to come down from my car.” Enoch said wanting to cry.

A lot of innocent people lost their lives to something they nothing about. Flourish herself pitied the children. Enoch wanted to know more about Flourish, since the previous night he met her, he just couldn’t stop thinking about her. He decided to start asking her some simple to complex questions.

“So what’s your name and where do you hail from.” He asked like a detective asking a criminal some questions.

“My name is Flourish and I hail from Edo state. I’m a pure Benin girl.” She said shyly.

“Are you married; I mean do you have a husband.”

“Sir my marital life cannot be justified.” She said feeling sober, she didn’t know how best to explain her marriage life.

“Are you having problems in your marriage?” He asked. “Sir I’ve been married twice.”

“Twice!” He exclaimed. “I don’t understand, please explain.”

“I got married to my first husband, David. His mother didn’t like me and so she did everything in her power to get me out. When I couldn’t give her son a child, she used that to her advantage, she set him up with another woman and meanwhile I’ve been trying my very best to have a child for him. Sometimes I would go to doctors and even pastors, I found it useless trying to have a child for him since he would be getting married to another woman. I decided to go stay with my uncle at Ibadan. He told me to move on with my life and look for someone to get married to. As God would have it I got sacked from my work and by mistake I bumped into a woman who introduced me to her brother to get married.” She paused to see how Enoch was responding. He was feeling touched by the story.

She cleared her throat and continued. “She told me that her brother had a company in Abuja and that she wanted to take me there. I accepted the offer and I fell in love with Joshua. He proposed and got married to me but after our marriage he started showing his other side, he comes home late at night very drunk, and he womanized as well. On one occasion when I tried to talk to him, he beat me so hard calling me all sorts of names. He told me to my face that he had a girl who already had 3 kids for him and that they were expecting a fourth child.”

“Those words pained me so hard; I started blaming nature for not been fair to me. He eventually brought the girl to my house and they were treating me like a slave. I was able to tolerate it but I was surprised when the children weren’t his. I left the house and decided to come to David’s house. He welcomed me with so much love but his new wife, Joan didn’t like that, and she invited a prophetess to lie to David that I was the cause of their childlessness. Unfortunately my husband believed the lie. He became so upset that he maltreated me; he made life so unbearable for me. I decided to leave the house, I didn’t want to go to my uncle house again so I decided to stay outside and that was where you saw me and saved me. Thank you again I really appreciate." She said crying. Enoch on the other hand couldn't believe what he just heard. He was speechless; he never knew the pain Flourish had passed through with both of her husbands. He felt pity for her and so he tried his best to comfort her.

"Flourish now I know your pain, I didn't understand you yesterday, I was just eager to give you comfort that I didn't care to know your encounter in this life, take it easy. Don't ever blame nature, my mother used to tell me that God sees us, he knows our suffering and he knows the time to give us happiness, just try to be patient." He said drawing himself closer to Flourish. He tried to clean her tears but he realized that the more he tried to clean her tears the more she cried.

"Well anyway, where do you intend to go, remember you can't stay here forever?"

"I know I've still not decided but I really want to get a job first at least for the meantime."

"Well I can help you get a job." He said whole heartedly. When she heard that, she refused instantly. She didn't want to have false hope again.

"No please don't bother yourself, I'm a tailor, I will just open a big shop, I don't want anything from you again." Enoch knew that Flourish was scared that maybe he might turn out to be like Joshua.

"Then at least let me give you some money to start a business." On hearing that, she became happy. She knew quiet well that she had no money to start a business, so she agreed.

"Well no problem, I will gladly accept the offer." She said shyly.

"Anyways, I'm a commissioner of the law; I work hand in hand with the governor of Lagos." "Really, wow you're so lucky." She said really excited.

"Yeah I know, he actually helped me get that position, we were close friends back then in the university, if you want I can help you become an officer."

Flourish liked the idea of becoming an officer. While she was still in school before Bella intervened in her life she had always wanted to be an officer of the law, but she had to deal with what nature had given her.

“You know that would be very nice, I’ve always wanted to be an officer of the law but because of the mistake I made in the past, I had to let go.” She said bringing her face down.

“I will talk to the governor; if he agrees then I will come back and tell you, but in the meantime start thinking of a place to go. Is there anybody here in Lagos that is a family member or a friend?” He asked a little worried about her wellbeing.

“I don’t think so. As far as I know, all my family members settled ties with me after an incident that occurred many years ago and I can’t remember having any family here in Lagos.” She said trying to recollect all her family members and family friends.

"No problem, I will talk to the governor and give you feedback tomorrow. But remember I only paid for just 3 days so you have to think fast."

Flourish had no idea on what to do next, she couldn't remember having any family member there in Lagos. While she was thinking, she quickly remembered Sarah. Sarah had been a friend to her mother; she always supported her mother in everything. Mrs. Sarah had been really helpful to Flourish but after the incident that occurred with her getting pregnant out of wedlock, Mrs. Sarah also broke ties with her. Flourish feared that Mrs. Sarah won't accept her but she just had to try her luck.

"I know of someone but I don't think she would accept me, but I will just try my luck." She said after a really long thought.

"No problem, just take care of yourself." He said as he stood up ready to go. "I will come back and give you feedback from the governor." he said as he placed his hand on her shoulder romantically. Flourish had a feeling that she had never felt before. It was as if she was falling for him already. Well what do you expect; he's a cute looking guy.

"Em, I will see you out." She said stammering. She walked Enoch out and planned to see Sarah. She quickly sprayed some perfume and left the hotel in search of Mrs. Sarah.

Sarah actually lived in Lagos and Flourish could vividly remember the house. While she was young, she usually came to pay a visit. She didn't know how successful Sarah had become now.

Sarah is now a secret agent working for some police force. At the time a woman was raped by her husband because she refused to have an intimate relationship with him, in the process the woman died. Rumors had it that the woman committed suicide but till now nobody knew what really caused it.

The woman family members had reported the case to the police; they just wanted to give justice to their poor daughter. They also wanted the case to be investigated and know what really happened because they don't believe their daughter was raped. Sarah had been on the case for over 2 weeks and all through her investigation she found out that the man was under the influence of alcohol and so was not in his right senses, he became so upset with his wife that he beat her so hard with a pestle, seeing that was not enough, he took a knife and stabbed her in her private part which made her bleed through her vagina. Through that everyone believed she was raped.

When the case was actually finalized, Sarah was paid a million naira, and she also had a catering business which fetched her lot of money.

She had a contract that involved baking a cake for the governor's wife. She was paid approximately 2.5 million for the cake. Her house was superb. Flourish couldn't stop herself from admiring the house.

She couldn't believe that Sarah would have gone far like this. The surroundings were decorated with flowers. "If this is how the outside of her house is, how will the inside look?" She asked rhetorically

Sarah noticed Flourish and decided to stop. She was actually on her way home. She came down from the car and walked towards Flourish.

"Madam what are you doing here." Sarah asked.

"Good…morning, good morning ma." Flourish said stammering. She was shivering but before she could allow Sarah to say anything else she got down on her knees crying.

"Mrs. Sarah please I know I was a bad child back then but now I've changed, I've realized what it means to be a woman. All the stress I've put into having kids for both of my husbands have made me open my eyes. I've gone through a lot ma, I would have lost my life yesterday, but I was saved by a man who booked a room for me. I have no place to go, please at least let me stay here. Please Mrs. Sarah, I promise I won't intrude in your privacy. In fact you can turn me into your housemaid if you want to but please let me have a place to rest my head." She said crying. Sarah could feel her pain, she decided to let her live with her.

"No problem. Get up let's go inside." She said trying to raise her up. She took her inside and brought a chilled glass of orange juice and gave it to her to drink.

"Flourish, I really do not understand what you are saying, but one thing is for sure you can stay. I don't have an objection towards that." Flourish felt secured as she narrated her story.

Sarah herself never knew that Flourish had suffered this much. She encouraged flourish to accept the offer and become an officer of the law.

Sarah had been like a mother; she talked to Flourish and gave her tips on how to be happy. She didn't try to encourage her to get into another relationship. In fact, she told her that relationships were meant to be built for some time.

She made her understand that a relationship that begins from just setup is bound to bring destruction at the end, but a relationship built on both love and understanding was bound to bring happiness and that true feeling of love.

Flourish could understand. None of the relationship she had was built on love and no wonder it lead to destruction at the end.

She began to think negatively upon herself that maybe she was never destined to fall in love and have a child of hers. This worried her the more. She wasn't able to bear a child; she had seen a lot of doctors but all still point out to the fact that her womb was badly damaged. She just prayed within her hearts that God would give her the ability to have a child of hers.

Chapter 8

Enoch had talked to the governor and he agreed. He was so happy that he couldn't wait to tell Flourish. He was actually falling in love with her. All through his life he has never fallen in love with any woman but this was his first.

He went to the hotel only to see her happy and packing her bags.

"I hope you have not gotten another job, because this one that you are happy. It's very suspicious." He said smiling as well.

"I have not gotten another job. Anyways what could be better than been an officer of the law? I'm happy because my family friend has agreed to take me in." she said with a lot of joy that all her dimples could be seen.

Enoch was also happy for her at least he won't be worried or scared about looking for a place for her to stay.

"Wow that's good news; I even have better news to tell you. I've spoken to the governor and he has agreed to take you in."

"Really" Flourish said shocked.

"Yes he agreed but you will have to come to the state house for some interview, he might not be the one to interview you but just come prepared." On hearing interview, Flourish heart beat faster than ever. She didn't know if she was qualified enough to fill in the vacant space. She had to stop school at a very crucial stage. "See Mr. Enoch I don't think I would be qualified for that job, I mean I didn't finish school." She said biting her finger.

"Don't worry, come tomorrow and see what God can do. I would be waiting for you at the state house gate come early and by the way you look beautiful."

That word beautiful made Flourish to start blushing. She was also falling for Enoch but she was hiding her feelings.

"Thank… thank you." She said stammering.

Enoch left the hotel and Flourish went to Sarah house. She didn't get the cold welcome she was expecting but she sure was happy to have a place to call home.

She told Sarah about the interview and how scared she was. Sarah calmed her down and practiced with her.

The next day Flourish hurriedly left the house and went to the state house. Luckily for her she saw Enoch patiently waiting for her. That was one thing she liked about him. He was always patient with her.

"You were really early, well let's go inside." Enoch said smiling at her.

She was going to be interviewed by the governor's wife. Mrs. Ague blessing was a beautiful but strict woman, she never played with her business. Her husband made her the minister of finance of Lagos and so everything about budgeting and finance was in her hands. Flourish entered into the office and was amazed but didn't want to be carried away.

"Good morning ma, I'm pleased to meet you." Flourish said shaking. Looking at the woman's face, it was more than enough for you to pee on yourself.

"Good morning how are you?" Blessing asked officially.

"I'm fine ma." Flourish replied sharply. They exchanged pleasantries and Flourish sat.

"I was sent on behalf of my husband, the governor to come and attend to you. Seeing that you are a decent girl and that you are looking for a position, I'm glad to announce to you that I will make you my Personal Assistance for Minister of Finance. You don't need to panic, I know you actually wanted to become an officer of the law but I'm sorry there are no more vacant spaces and I'm also in need of help with the work I'm doing. Please reason with me, you will have your own office, your own personal car and driver, you don't have to worry about money. To me money is not a problem." Mrs. Blessing said.

She was only doing this for her own selfish reason. But not because that she is strict doesn't mean that she was wicked. She also had a heart of gold. Enoch had informed her about flourish past life and so she pitied her and decided to give her the job. Flourish also liked the idea. She couldn't believe that she would be the Personal Assistance to the Minister of Finance and the governor's wife for that matter.

"I have heard your story and I feel pity for you that is why I gave you this position because you truly deserve it." Blessing said soft heartedly.

For the first time she was speaking so nice. She was known for her strictness.

"I will show you to your office." Blessing said requesting for a handshake as they both stood up. She took Flourish to her new office. It was very beautiful; it was really big with an air conditioner and comfortable office desks. It was exactly what she had dreamt of. She had always wanted to sit in her own office, with her legs crossed and being a boss.

She couldn't thank Mrs. Blessing enough for giving her such an opportunity. She told her all she needed to know. Flourish on the other hand couldn't wait to tell Enoch all that had happened.

After all the proceedings were done, Flourish went to meet Enoch who was eager to know how it went.

"So how did it go?" Enoch asked. A little scared.

"Well it wasn't what I expected but she made me her PA." Flourish said really happy. Enoch couldn't hide his excitement anymore. He hugged her; he had been waiting for that moment when he would cuddle her. Flourish wanted to tell him about her feelings but she just decided to keep quiet.

"Am…am I did not intend to do that. I only did it because I was very excited." He said stammering and clearing his throat on the process. After sometime he began smiling. He held her hand and started walking towards the outside door, but they were stopped by Blessing.

"Flourish here is a cheque, cash it and use the money to buy some new clothes, shoes, handbags and some other basic necessities you may need for work." She said handing over the cheque to Flourish.

Flourish looked at the cheque and saw the sum of 500 thousand naira. She couldn't demonstrate how happy she was. She begged Enoch to take her to a shopping mall which he did without any hesitation.

The next day flourish started working. On some occasions, Blessing would give her the permission to handle some budgets.

One of such budgets Flourish made was the generation of electricity to neighboring areas. That budget made the governor a little bit upset because he was going to spend a lot of money which he never intended to spend.

Mrs. Blessing herself was delighted with the budget she created. She praised her, even Sarah was happy with flourish, Sarah's family praised her so much and they continued to give her the best.

Enoch on the other hand was just thinking about how he would propose to Flourish. He knew all that she had gone through with her previous marriage and because of that she might be forced to say no, but he was still willing to take his chance.

He wanted to date her, take her out and make her feel loved. He himself couldn't believe that the same distressed woman he met sitting on the bare floor some days ago was now a personal assistant to the governor's wife. He went to Sarah's house. He just wanted to tell her he felt about her. Since that day he met her under the hot blazing sun, he couldn't stop thinking about her.

As he got to the house, he met one of Sarah's children trimming the flowers. Benedetto was Sarah's first child and only daughter. She was 18 years and was in 300 levels, studying mechanical engineering. She had always been the apple of her father's eyes as she was much focused on her studies and never got distracted.

Other children of her age grade would have already been in a relationship. Though it's normal to have a boyfriend or girlfriend, she never got interested in such relationships, because her main goal was to become a Mechanical Engineer. Enoch liked the way Sarah trained her daughter. He wished his children could be just like her.

"Good morning, nice flowers." Enoch said.

"Oh good morning sir, are you here to see Aunty Flourish? She's inside." She said in a rush. She already knew why he was here. Just to see his love. Enoch didn't hesitate to go inside, he couldn't wait to tell flourish how he felt about her. Luckily for him he saw Sarah coming down the stairs.

"Ah Enoch you are here, this one that you came this morning, I hope all is well?" Sarah asked.

"All is well ma; I only came to see Flourish." He said shyly. Sarah already knew where he was heading to. Flourish had told her earlier that she had feelings for Enoch, so Sarah knew that Enoch was also falling for her.

"No problem, she's in her room upstairs, I will just call her." Sarah said smiling as she went to call Flourish. Few minutes later, she was back with Flourish who was also blushing at the sight of Enoch.

"Flourish is here already, so I will just leave you two love birds to discuss and express each other's feelings." Sarah said as she quickly dashed into the kitchen to get a glass of water and up to her room.

"Well…am…well I was hoping I could take you out to see the movies, go for shopping then maybe go for dinner…am whatever you girls do." He said stammering. He was feeling too shy to talk to her face to face.

“That sounds quite inviting, I was already getting bored and this is an opportunity to leave the house, you know what, let me go and change and then we can go out.” Flourish said happily that she was finally going out on a date with her love.

She quickly put on her finest clothes. She couldn’t believe that she was already 25. All her life experiences had made her forget herself. She couldn’t be more thankful to God for bringing Enoch into her life, ever since he came into her life; he changed her for the better.

She got dressed quickly and came downstairs to meet him. Enoch didn’t realize how beautiful Flourish was, he couldn’t wait to hug and kiss her.

“Well, how do I look?” Flourish asked smiling.

“Am…you look very beautiful.” Enoch couldn’t get his eyes off her body that he felt like romancing her body.

“Can we go?” Flourish asked sensing that Enoch couldn’t get his eyes off her.

"Yes of course." Enoch took her to the cinema to see a movie. At that time, they were watching a romantic movie. After that he took her to a shopping mall to shop. He was ready to spend on her because he believed that she was the one he was destined to be with.

He had bought a beautiful diamond ring; he was ready to propose to her. He couldn't hide his feeling anymore. He just wanted to pour his heart towards her. He had arranged with the manager of the restaurant to decorate and keep a table for two.

Flourish herself was amazed with the way Enoch arranged everything. The table, the restaurant and everything were just so beautiful. They ordered for some chicken. Flourish suspected that Enoch wanted to say something because he was kind of distracted.

"Mr. Enoch, I hope all is well, why are you clumsy?" She asked really concerned.

'No, it's nothing, it's just…, and it's just nothing. Get back to your food." He became so scared because he had no idea on how he could propose to her. He decided to let go of the fear. He knelt down, looked into her eyes, held her hand and placed it on his chest. Then he brought out a small box from his breast pocket, opened it and brought out a ring.

"Flourish since that day I met you under the sun, I couldn't stop thinking about you, I don't know why I feel this way but for sure I know this is love, I've never felt this way towards any women but now I feel this way towards you. Flourish I really love you, I sure do. I love you so much and I don't think I would be able to live without you. I am not a man without you, Flourish please, please I'm begging you, will you marry me?"

Enoch just stared at Flourish; her facial expression was filled with doubts. He feared she may not agree. Flourish on the other hand loved him but she also feared that she may not be able to bear children for him.

"Enoch, I love you too but I can't bear a child for you, what is love in a marriage when there is no child in it? Despite Even I can't live without you, I love you so much but I'm trying to see the future. I don't want this marriage to turn out to be like my previous marriage that is why I don't want to accept it." She said as some tears dropped down her cheeks.

Enoch was expecting to get such response from her but he didn't want to be defeated by her disappointment.

"Flourish what are you saying? I love you, I don't care if we don't have a child, I just want to live with you, I want you to be by my side, please Flourish don't disappoint me." He said trying to convince her. He really loved her.

"I'm a barren woman, please find another woman, I don't want to give you false hope, I want you to be blessed with children. I just pity you. I've learnt to accept the fact that I won't be able to bear children. I can't imagine myself going through that emotional trauma again."

Enoch knew what she was going through. To him he didn't care if he had a child or not, he just wanted Flourish by his side, he loved her and he wasn't ready to let her go.

"You know, I don't really care if I have a child or not, I just want you. I don't really care if we are barren or what the world may say about us. Flourish please marry me." He said shivering.

Flourish had no choice; she couldn't just loose Enoch like that.

"Yes I will marry you; I wouldn't want to lose you for the world." She said as some tears flowed down her cheeks.

Enoch didn't hesitate to place the ring on her finger. Immediately, he got up and kissed her. Flourish realized how romantic Enoch was. The way he kissed her was a moment she couldn't forget. Everybody at the restaurant started clapping and wishing them a happy married life. After that Enoch drove Flourish back home and she immediately went to show Sarah her fingers.

"Ma look I'm engaged." On hearing that Sarah couldn't hold her tears anymore. They were actually tears of joy.

"It is well with you, I just hope that it goes smoothly and that you guys have no porthole in your relationship." Sarah said encouraging Flourish. This reminded Flourish of her parents. It has been really long since she saw her family.

She knew that if she goes back, her parents may never accept her. To months into Enoch and Flourish's courtship, Flourish decided to see her parents. She wanted to go with Enoch because she knew he would be there to defend her

"Enoch I want to go home, I want to see my family members and hug my siblings, it has been really long since I last saw them." Enoch himself wanted to see Flourish's parents. He wanted to discuss with them, the marriage preparations.

"No problem, we'll take a leave from our jobs and go on this journey." He said as he kissed her. Flourish became scared as she packed her belongings. She was no longer living with Sarah but with Enoch. Sarah had encouraged her to start living with Enoch so that they could know and understand each other and prepare for their marital life.

"What's the problem darling, you seem disturbed." He asked really concerned because she was not always like that.

"It's my family, it's been a long time since we've seen each other, I don't think they may want to see my face." She said almost wanting to cry. Enoch could understand what she was going through. "Don't worry, I'm sure they must have forgiven you by now, let's go." In not less than 30 minutes, they packed their belongings and were heading to Husain. Husain was the name of her village she was brought up. Though she hailed from Edo state, her father had a land in Husain where he built a house and moved all his family members

When they entered the village, Flourish saw a lot of changes. Flourish couldn't recognize anything at all. She began to wonder if she would be able to recognize her family house.

"This placed has really changed. It seems like this place has developed since I left. In fact I don't think I would be able to recognize my house again." Flourish said looking round the village from the window trying to locate her house.

"Of course it must have changed, it's been really long. I mean it's been 10 years ago." Enoch said smiling at her. He assured her that they were going to find her house. While she was still carrying out her search, she caught sight of her dad's house. It hadn't change at all.

"That's my house." Flourish said pointing towards a half demolished house. She was even ashamed to call it her house. Enoch packed at the front of the house. Flourish mother who was sitting at the passage entrance caught sight of her daughter and ran as fast as she could to hold her daughter. Even with her old age, she was still able to move those legs. She was barely fifty years of age.

"Flourish my child." She said touching her face and crying as well.

"Mummy good afternoon." The Two love birds greeted.

"Good afternoon my children please don't hesitate to come in." she said sniffing. She was so overjoyed with joy that she didn't want the kids to see her cry. "Mummy I really missed you, that is why I came back, where is daddy?" She asked looking round.

"Flourish your father is dead." JUSTINA said almost wanting to cry.

"What?" flourish screamed "What do you mean mama? That papa is dead." Flourish said not believing.

"Yes my child, your father died a year after you left, he couldn't handle the shame, and because all the elders were laughing at him that he couldn't train his child well, your father had hypertension as a result of too much thinking and depression he had, he just left us like that my child." she said crying. She couldn't handle the trauma anymore.

"So I'm the cause of my father's death." Flourish said crying.

"Calm down my dear. Things happen for a reason, maybe if your father had been alive; we wouldn't have been together by now. Just take control over yourself." Enoch said trying to comfort her as he helped her clean her tears.

Those words brought up her feelings back. Flourish after reconciling with all her family members later introduced Enoch as her fiancé. She told her mother about all the life experiences she had with her previous marriages.

Her mother comforted her and reassured her that this wedding with Enoch was going to bring her a lot of happiness. She also told her that her marriage with Enoch was going to bring her fruitful and abundant blessing. They both chorused amen when she said that.

They stayed in the village for about a week and later went back to Lagos. Flourish couldn't wait to get married to Enoch. They have been courting each other for quite long now. She still couldn't believe that she found happiness again.

Chapter 9

Flourish and Enoch's wedding bells were already ringing. Preparations for their wedding were already on ground. Solomon had promised Enoch that he would sponsor his wedding. He wanted it to be one in a million and that everyone would be aware of it.

Flourish couldn't believe her eyes, she was going to get married again and this time to her true lover. Enoch on the other hand couldn't believe that the same distressed woman he saw under the hot blazing sun was going to be his wife.

It was too hard to believe but in all he gave thanks to God. Inside the church as Flourish walked down the aisle, she began to radiate in her white sparkling wedding gown. Her beauty was even multiplied with the light make up she put on. As she marched forward majestically, Enoch heart almost jumped out of his body. To him he was seeing a beautiful angel approaching him.

As she walked towards Enoch and the priest, Enoch couldn't stop himself from staring at her, she was so beautiful that her beauty was more than enough to take away anyone's sorrow.

The entire guest, among which was the governor, his wife, her colleagues from the ministry were all there to support and cheer her up on this very special day of her life.

The bishop turned to Enoch and asked him. "Mr. Enoch, do you take Flourish here to be your lovable wife in good and in bad time, in sickness and in healthy life, in happiness and in sorrow, that you shall forever be with her till death do you part." "Yes I do." Enoch replied sharply. He was so excited.

The bishop then turned to flourish and asked her the same question. " Flourish, do you take Enoch to be your lovable husband in good and bad times, in sickness and in healthy life, in happiness and in sorrow that you shall forever be with him until death do you apart."

"Yes I do." Flourish replied.

"I now pronounce you husband and wife, you may kiss the bride." They didn't waste a single second before they kissed each other.

After the church wedding, the reception followed at whispering palm hotel and resorts, Badgerys. People that flourish had never expected to come actually came. Even the president of Nigeria was present at the wedding. Suleiman and flora weren't left out at all. They were also present at the wedding.

The wedding was fabulous, it was a grand celebration. After the wedding, Sarah escorted the wedded couples to their house. She had booked a hotel room in drolly sight at Dubai. She wanted them to enjoy themselves. She arranged for their visas and they were going to leave the following week.

Flourish loved her wedding night; she never knew how romantic her husband was. He bought her a Lexus 390 as her wedding gift. Flourish couldn't express how happy she was to receive such a gift.

Every day, she would thank God for bringing Enoch into her life; he had made her life a precious jewel.

The following week, they took their flight to Dubai to spend their honeymoon. While in the plane, flourish couldn't stop talking about Dubai.

"You know what honey; Dubai is the perfect place for us to spend our honeymoon. I heard that there is a desert there, and some other fun tourist sites." She said excited as she looked at the world from above.

"Yes we are going to have so much fun there in Dubai." Enoch replied. He was just smiling at her. Flourish never knew that she was going to find true happiness again.

On getting to Dubai, the two couples were amazed at the environment they found themselves in. "Dubai is really a nice place to spend our honeymoon." Enoch said holding her hand. He knew if he let her go, then over excitement will take over her and then she might get lost.

They boarded a cab that would take them to drolly site. While in the car they saw a lot of beautiful sites, Dubai was really a beautiful place.

They went to the hotel booked for them to spend their honeymoon, as usual; they were amazed with the room. It was spacious, beautifully arranged. The bed was evenly decorated with red roses. It was as if the manager of the hotel intentionally decorated the room just to make their honeymoon special.

They were lost in the beauty of the room, that they had forgotten the main reason they were there.

Flourish started feeling down because of her barrenness. She was lost in thoughts; she didn't want to be rejected by Enoch. She wanted him to be happy and have children. Enoch noticed that flourish was lost in thoughts, so he decided to know what she was thinking.

"Honey, what's going on in your mind?" He asked concerned as he drew himself closer to her.

"Nothing, it's nothing. I was just admiring the room." She said lying almost wanting to cry but held the rain from falling.

"It's crystal clear from your facial expression that you are telling a lie. You are obviously thinking about how you are going to have a child, right." He said fully confident, knowing what was on her mind.

"Please sit down." He said, trying to take her to the bed.

"You know my sweetheart, God has a way of turning bitterness into sweetness, I'm sure God has seen all you went through and he is going to reward you. I know that children have a way of strengthening the bond between couples but I don't have a problem if we do not have children. As long as there is life, there is hope. Love can change anything no matter the circumstances that befalls us." Enoch said kissing her forehead.

Flourish managed to smile after he had teased her a little. She was really thankful to God to have given her such a husband. Someone who would go to any extent just to make her smile was indeed wonderful.

They spent the rest of their honeymoon visiting many tourists' sites. They went to the Sahara deserts. Some other Amusements Park, a pool at the hotel, a love garden, limited to only couples and those in serious love relationship. After their honeymoon in Dubai was over, they came back to Nigeria. Flourish became scared again, that she still hadn't heard the good news that she was pregnant, she spent 2 months at Dubai and yet no news. She started praying to God to give her children. She didn't want Enoch to be childless. He was a good man and so deserved good things.

Enoch also noticed that she had started crying again, he didn't know how best to convince her but he just prayed to God to get rid of Flourish problem.

Three months after they had arrived in Nigeria, Flourish became sick. She had complained of having high fever and headache but Enoch didn't give it more concern. He just told her to rest and that the headache would go

Unluckily for him, he left the house very early in the morning to attend a very important meeting when he was called that Flourish had been rushed to the hospital for reasons he knew nothing about.

Could it be what we've all been waiting for? He was driving like a hungry lion that was pursuing his prey. You can imagine how many minutes he took to get to the hospital.

He wondered what the problem was; he was scared because he didn't want anything bad to happen to her. He loved her so much and he wasn't willing to let her go just like that.

As he got to the hospital, he met her in the emergency room; some nurses were with her trying to attend to her. "Nurse, how is my wife, what happened to her, why is she here." He asked trying to catch his breath.

"Sir the doctor isn't around but we've given her some pain killers that will reduce the pain, so you can take her home and take good care of her." The nurse said and left the scene. Enoch looked at flourish; she was lying on the bed unconsciously. He immediately took her home.

When she finally woke up, she was surprised seeing Enoch in front her. She couldn't remember anything happening to her but she remembered Enoch leaving the house for his meeting.

"Honey what are you doing here? Aren't you supposed to be at work?" She asked still feeling headache as she touched her head and trying to get up from the bed.

"Calm down, you have to rest; I will explain everything to you when you've rested." He said trying to make her sleep. He gave her some paracetamol and told her to rest.

The next morning he prepared her favorite food, pounded yam and black soup, since she was not strong enough to cook.

The aroma of the food made her rush to the bathroom to throw up. Enoch wondered what was wrong with his wife. He began to worry if her sickness had turned worse. He helped her in washing her face and took her to the room.

"Honey, what's wrong with me?" Flourish asked almost wanting to cry.

"There is nothing wrong with you, you are perfectly fine." Enoch said trying to comfort her as he helped her clean her tears. She asked for some bread and omelet, which Enoch didn't hesitate to prepare. He just wanted Flourish to eat.

He then left for work, after giving her a kiss and telling her to rest. As soon as he left, Flourish headache began again and she decided to rest. She refused to take any pain killers. She couldn't even pick any of Enoch's call. He was trying to reach her to find out how she was doing.

He became scared that maybe something bad had happened to her. He began to remember the adage that says. “Good things never last.” He wasn’t comfortable working anymore as the thoughts of Flourish’s illness took over his working hours.

“How can I just let go of such a pretty damsel like Flourish, I haven’t even enjoyed her and now this is already happening, why can’t good things last, why does flourish have to suffer like this.” He said talking to himself.

Meanwhile, Flourish managed to prepare dinner. Because of how tired and weak she was, she forgot that the bean was on fire for over 2 hours, by that time, it was already burnt. She only remembered that the bean was on fire when the aroma of the burnt beans had started ruminating round the house.

She rushed to off it and she became scared because she thought that Enoch was going to yell at her. “What am I going to do now?” She said holding her head. She had no choice but to go back to bed. He was her husband after all so he was bound to yell at her sometimes.

When Enoch came home, he knocked for over an hour but Flourish didn't hear him. He even yelled out her name but she still didn't come out. He even called her phone number but she still didn't pick his calls. Enoch began to wonder what was wrong with her. He feared that she may have fainted.

He decided to knock at their room window, maybe she could be there. He thought to himself. He knocked really hard this time and she woke up. She quickly rushed to open the door for her husband. "Oh honey, welcome." She said yawning.

Enoch became angry but he didn't want to blame her, it wasn't her fault at all. "What have you been doing? I've been knocking for over an hour now, I was even calling you but you didn't pick any of my calls." He said a little angry.

"Honey I'm sorry, it's this headache, I've also been trying to rest, I even managed to prepare dinner for you." She said with the little strength in her.

"Baby, let me take you to the hospital, this headache of yours is getting worse." Enoch said really concerned. He was super worried about her health. He couldn't help but wonder what the problem was.

"No honey, there is no need to go to the hospital, I'm absolutely fine, it's just a slight headache." She said trying to switch away from the topic.

She quickly took off his clothes and told him to freshen up. She then went to serve him the burnt beans. Enoch was annoyed at the sight of the burnt beans. He didn't know what was wrong with his wife; he didn't want to complain about the food because he didn't want to hurt her feelings. Before he could sip a spoon into his mouth, Flourish rushed to the bathroom again to throw up.

This was the second time she was vomiting and it began to dawn in Enoch that Flourish was seriously ill. All hell was let loose when she fainted after coming out of the bathroom. Enoch rushed to where she laid and started calling her name.

He quickly rushed her to the hospital; he was just horning like a mad dog. He didn't want to lose Flourish. As soon as he got to the hospital he started sweating profusely, as he watched as Flourish was been carried into the emergency room. He started praying to God that all should go smoothly and that Flourish should be safe.

Few minutes into waiting, a doctor came to where Enoch was. As Enoch sighted the doctor, he began to shiver.

“Sir we’ve done some tests on her, she’s okay, she only had malaria and congratulations, she’s 4 weeks pregnant. We have given her some malaria drugs and some pain killers, she will be okay.” The doctor said smiling.

Enoch couldn’t believe what he just heard. The same woman that couldn’t bear a child for her previous husbands was now pregnant. It was too hard to believe but in all he thanked God.

He didn’t know how best to break the news to Flourish. He knew she might not believe she was pregnant. I mean a woman who was told by different doctors that her womb was badly damaged and won’t be able to conceive will definitely get a shock, and it will take a whole lot of love to get her to believe.

As he entered the room, tears of joy flowed down his cheeks, he was so happy. He stood beside the bed and watched her beautiful face. He began to agree with the adage that "God blesses those who bless others." God has really heard all of Flourish's prayers and He has finally heard his prayers too.

As she woke up, she saw Enoch smiling, it was then she knew something was going on. She just hoped it was good news.

"Honey what happened, what's making you smile?" flourish said as she managed to get up. "Sweet heart, how do I tell you that…that we…we are going to become parents, you will become a mother and I will be a father." Enoch said holding her hand and kissing her forehead.

Flourish couldn't believe what she just heard, a lot of doctors had told her that she was infertile and that she can never have a child again. She wondered what could have happened.

"What are you saying? Don't play a joke on me." Flourish said still not believing.

"I'm not lying, the doctor said you are 4 weeks pregnant, it was hard to believe but I had to thank God for blessing us." Flourish couldn't thank God enough. She started crying but it was all tears of joy. Indeed it was a miracle. A barren woman would soon become a mum; it was too hard to believe.

She hugged Enoch and gave him a kiss. She was discharged and Enoch started taking good care of her. The news of Flourish's pregnancy reached the office.

Mrs. Blessing who already knew about Flourish previous life was so happy, she couldn't believe that Flourish was pregnant but in all she joined them to thank God. All of Flourish colleagues and some of the ministers at work threw a small party to congratulate the soon to be parents. Mrs. Sarah also got the news, she was so happy for her. She congratulated her and gave her some baby pampers. This was such a happy occasion for Flourish.

At the time flourish was pregnant, her beauty was already defoliating but Enoch never stopped loving her. He kept on showering her with all the love he could give her; he always gave her words of encouragement. On one occasion, Flourish went to the mirror to look at her protruding belly and her face. She started saying to herself. "I'm very ugly; I don't think my husband still loves me." She said really upset. Enoch overheard her and went to meet her. He held her by her waist and said to her. "Honey you are still beautiful, don't let yourself be defeated by the way you look like in the mirror. You are very beautiful, you still haven't changed at all and I want you to still remember that I love you." He said kissing her

Those words made Flourish feel happy again. She was quite sure that her husband loved her.

Flourish's pregnancy didn't deprive her from going to work, she worked hard but Blessing wanted her to rest so she gave her a leave when she was 6 months pregnant.

Flourish had told Enoch to accompany her to the ultra-scan clinic. She wanted to know the gender and position of her baby.

Flourish was really keen to know the gender of her baby. In most typical Nigerian homes, a male child is a symbol of love, and most men prefer to have male children rather than female children.

Enoch wasn't that type of guy. He didn't mind not having kids, not to talk of having male children. Well at first Flourish doubted the fact that her husband didn't care about the gender of her child so she decided to ask him about it.

"Baby, would you like it if the baby turns out to be a girl." Flourish asked skeptically. Enoch couldn't believe that she was asking such a question. To him he didn't care if he had a boy or a girl, so long as he had a child coming his way.

"But you know quite well that I really don't care if we have a girl or boy. I will make do with which ever child that comes." Flourish felt relax after hearing her husband say that. Sometimes she usually wonders what she could do without her darling husband.

Chapter 10

While in the ultra-scan clinic, they didn't know what joy they were going to meet there. After about 30 minutes, the doctor came out smiling.

Doctor Annabel had been flourish doctor since the day she arrived at the hospital after she fainted. Doctor Annabel was a gynecologist, which had been her family's business. Her dad was a gynecologist and he opened the door to give her insight.

She had made a vow to herself to always protect women and their children. This was because of an incident that happened many years ago. Her father had brought her to the hospital when she was 10 years old because her mother and her other siblings travelled and she couldn't stay at home all by herself.

A woman who was due for delivery and was pregnant for triplets came, she came with her son, a 5 year old boy. She was waiting patiently for the doctor who was to give her admission into the hospital. She was told that doctor Phillips wasn't around and that he was on his leave. All the doctors at that moment were very busy and no one could attend to her.

Young Annabel was just sitting there watching the poor woman. She wished she could help her but she was just a little kid. She later made friend with the young boy.

When the woman started complaining of abdominal pain, she fell down to the floor and started bleeding from her private part. Some nurses quickly rushed her to the emergency room. When the ladies labour progress, the nurses became confused because the woman was unable to push.

The babies were not making any move to come out. They started saying to themselves that if the doctor handling her case was around he would have booked for a caesarian surgery. They were so confused that they couldn't see the weakness in the woman's eyes. She was already weak and she was groaning.

The triplets in her were already suffocating as their legs were managing to come out. It was then one of the nurses went to call Doctor Mario, Annabel's dad. By the time she was taken to the operating room, she had already kicked the bucket with the triplets still in her.

The young boy on hearing some nurses talking about the death of his mother burst into a loud cry. This caught the attention of Dr. Mario who tried to calm the boy down. That incident made Annabel have a strong flare for women. She made sure that every pregnant woman in her custody always got the best treatment.

When she realized that flourish was pregnant with twins, she made a decision to take care of her and her babies.

"You don't have to worry sir; your babies are kicking well." Dr. Annabel said smiling. Enoch didn't understand what the doctor was saying, what does she mean by babies.

"Please doctor I don't understand what you are saying." Enoch asked looking at Flourish whose facial expressions was mixed with happiness.

"Your babies have good heart beats and in few months to come they will join the both of you." Flourish herself was confused; she didn't understand what the doctor meant by babies, she began to think that maybe she was carrying twins in her womb.

"Doctor please can you be very specific in your words? I really don't understand." Enoch asked really confused.

"I'm only saying that your wife here is carrying 2 adorable children in her womb, and from the scan we have here, you are expecting a boy and a girl." She said very happy.

Flourish was overweighed with joy. She couldn't believe that she was carrying 2 children in her womb. She was once considered a barren woman before and now she would be known as a mother of twins.

"God has really been great; God has shown me what it is to be a woman." She said to Enoch. They were so overjoyed with happiness. While they were going home she started reflecting on her previous life, how she was maltreated in Joshua's house and how David treated her like nobody

"God is really wonderful; he knows a way of turning bitterness into sweetness." Flourish said in her mind.

Three months later, Enoch was called for a security meeting in the governor's villa. His work as an officer had really brought him closer to the government.

He handled cases of security because at the moment, terrorist had threatened the peace of the state. Before Enoch left the house, he kissed Flourish and promised to be back early.

As he got to the venue, his phone rang. It was Dr. Annabel. She wanted to tell him that Flourish was in labour and that she needed to be operated on. After Enoch had left the house, Flourish called Annabel that she was feeling some unusual pains in her lower abdomen. Doctor Annabel told her to come to the hospital immediately so that they could keep a close eye on her.

Flourish got to the hospital and few minutes after she was admitted, she entered into labor.

Dr. Annabel didn't want anything that will affect the safety of the babies so she recommended that she be operated on. She quickly called Enoch so that he could fill some necessary forms. When Enoch saw her name on the phone, his heart began to beat faster than ever.

He was scared that maybe something bad had happened to his wife. A lot of questions kept on flashing through his head as he picked the call.

"Hello doctor, what's the problem?" He asked fervently

"Mr. Enoch you will have to come to the hospital immediately, your wife needs to be operated on and you need to fill some forms." She said in a rush as she cut the phone.

Enoch started rushing to the hospital. He was so scared; he was just praying that the operation be carried out successfully.

As he got to the hospital, a nurse walked up to him and gave him a form to fill, which he did immediately. He asked the nurse where Flourish was being operated and she took him there. As he entered the room he saw flourish lying down, she was on a drip. I guess she's probably resting after the surgery. He said in his thoughts.

He turned to his left only to see his two beautiful children lying in a cradle. He went to where they were, and took them into his hands. He then took them to where Flourish was lying and placed them side by side her. He never knew how God could be so kind, he did not just bless him with one child but two.

Few days later she was discharged, both Flourish and Enoch started thinking of names to call their children. After some close thoughts they both decided to call the children, Francis and Frances.

Flourish loves the name and it really fits the children. Enoch wanted the dedication ceremony of his children to be grand. He wanted the whole world to know that a barren woman whom was rejected by many is now the mother of twins. He told his parents and relatives about the good news. He didn't also hesitate to tell flourish's mother and siblings. Everyone was so happy.

He did the reception at his house. All the ministers, governors, colleagues of both Enoch and Flourish were present to join them to thank God for giving them twins.

David, who had been after problems with Joan, heard that Flourish had put to birth to adorable twins. He couldn't believe that Flourish already had children. He wished he had never driven flourish away.

After Flourish had left the house, Joan continued showing her other sides. She would leave the house very early in the morning and return late at night.

David had complained to his mother that he couldn't tolerate Joan's attitude anymore. Justin always supported Joan and encouraged her to do anything to have a child.

David decided to go to the hospital to find out if he was infertile or not. To his upmost surprise he was very fertile. It began to dawn in him that Joan was the one infertile. He followed her one day to monitor her movement; he only regretted ever getting married to her.

He saw her collecting money from a young guy just to spend the rest of the day with him. He became so angry that he felt like beating her to death.

When she eventually got home, she started behaving innocent, unknowingly to her, David already knew about her whereabouts. David's mother received her with so much keenness.

"My daughter, how did it go?" She asked unaware of the crime her fake daughter in law had committed. "

"Joan where are you've been." David asked in a fit of rage.

"Where else would I have been, I went to see the doctor and you won't believe that he has found a remedy to our childlessness." On hearing childlessness, David got up from his chair and in a fit of rage pounce on her and started beating her.

David's mother tried separating them but to no avail. He was very angry. "You this evil woman, you made me throw away the woman I once loved. You separated me from my true lover, what kind of a woman are you?" David said in a fit of rage as he continued to beat her. After sustaining some deserved injuries, she packed her things and left the house. His only mistake which he still regretted till now was ever falling for Joan.

When he heard that Flourish had given birth to twins, he couldn't believe his ears and he only regretted ever throwing her away. Well there is a saying that goes. "You don't value what you have until you lose it." The saying was actually applicable to David. He didn't know how precious Flourish was until she left him.

David after inquiring the location of where the dedication ceremony would be held went to ask for forgiveness. When he got to the house he saw both Enoch and Flourish dressed in their beautiful white laces and carrying their adorable children in their hands. They were both smiling which showed how happy they were.

He regretted ever making such a nasty mistake, he could have been the one in Enoch's place but everything happens for a reason. He ran to where Flourish was and went on his knees.

Flourish was shocked seeing David; she didn't want any of her past life to come back again. She was done with her childless life and now she has chosen to accept the gift of nature and appreciate what it is to be a woman.

Before she could alert Enoch to take David away, David started talking. "Flourish please

I've come back, I've learnt my lesson. I was just blind folded by that stupid Joan that I didn't see the goodness in your heart. She was the one who was barren, I couldn't tolerate her attitude anymore and I made her pack out of the house. I heard people say you gave birth to twins, I couldn't believe and I had to come see for myself. Please I love you and I'm here to ask for your mercy. Please forgive me." David said almost wanting to cry.

Flourish hated the word love coming out from David's mouth. "It's too late, now I'm married, I've left my past life behind, and I don't love you anymore, please just go and leave me alone." Flourish said very angrily but she didn't want it to ruin her mood.

Enoch was disgusted at the sight of David. He was ruining the happiness of the crowd and everyone was on ground to see if the innocent lovable flourish would choose to go back to her evil husband.

"Young man, please leave. You have no business with Flourish again so it would best for everyone if you could just leave." Enoch said almost wanting to punch himself but he withdrew knowing fully well that his reputation was at stake.

David had no choice but to leave. He was actually ruining their happiness. It was such a happy occasion and so he couldn't afford to make them frown.

On his way out, he noticed how everyone was looking at him with disgust. He didn't care at all because now he was hopeless. He had no reason to live anymore and so he decided to commit suicide. It was one of his neighbors that rushed him to the hospital,

According to the report given by his neighbor, David came home looking dejected. He stood outside looking up at the sky for over 2 minutes and then he rushed into the kitchen to get a knife. He ran outside quickly and started shouting rhetorically to himself.

"I have no reason to live now; the love of my life has been taking away from me.' Those were his last words and then he stabbed himself to death. His neighbor who had witnessed everything couldn't summon enough courage to stop him.

David's mother was informed about the death of her son. She knew such a thing was going to happen so she had no one to blame but her terrible self.

The incident that happened with David didn't stop the dedication ceremony of Flourish adorable twins. In fact she was unaware of David's death. The celebration brought up the emotions of Mrs. Blessing. She was really grateful to God for blessing flourish with children.

The Flourish that was once barren was now a mother of twins. It was too hard to believe but the news became a headline in the newspaper and gossip to those lazy and busy bodied women.

Mrs. Blessing wanted to do something special for Flourish and so after her maternity leave, she invited her to her office. On the call, Mrs. Blessing sounded very urgent. This worried Flourish who felt that maybe she was going to be sacked. She told Enoch about the call but he only advised her to take to the call.

After giving her kids the necessary feeding they needed, she went to see Mrs. Blessing. She made sure she dressed beautifully and official. Even though she had put to birth, her shape and face hadn't change at all. She always made sure she looked her best and her husband supported her as well. He loved her so much and he wanted her to look her best.

She entered the office looking shy and scared because of how serious Mrs. Blessing face looked.

"Good morning ma." Flourish greeted. "God morning my dear, How are the kids." Mrs. Blessing asked smiling.

"They are fine ma." Flourish replied coldly.

"I'm sure you're wondering why I called you here." Blessing said. "Yes ma." She replied sharply

"I have seen all the good deeds you've done and I really think that I should reward you." She said smiling. Flourish began to wonder what reward awaited her.

“I have decided that I would make you the Minister of Finance, I really think I should rest a little. You know that I really trust you and so I’m putting you in charge of all that that there is with my business.” Flourish couldn’t believe her ears. She was now the Minister of Finance.

Flourish’s life had really changed for the better. She couldn’t believe that she had come this far. All her life experiences had made her loose hope in life but at the end of it all she was favored and she learnt that there is joy in being a woman.

www.ingramcontent.com/pod-product-compliance
Lightning Source LLC
LaVergne TN
LVHW010557160826
845677LV00013B/3158

* 9 7 9 8 3 7 0 4 3 8 1 2 7 *